Lock Down Publications and Ca$h
Presents

I0564659

SAVAGE FAMILY EMPIRE

Power
A Black Mafia Origin Story

Part 2

Written By
PRINCE A. TAUHID

First Edition 2025

Printed in the United States of America

This is a work of fiction. Names, characters, places, and incidents either are products of the author's imagination or are used fictitiously. Any similarity to actual events or locales or persons, living or dead, is entirely coincidental.

Lock Down Publications
P.O. Box 944
Stockbridge, GA 30281
www.lockdownpublications.com

Like our page on Facebook: Lock Down Publications
www.facebook.com/lockdownpublications.ldp

Stay Connected with Us!

Text **LOCKDOWN** to 22828 to stay up-to-date with new releases, sneak peaks, contests and more...

Like our page on Facebook:
Lock Down Publications

Join Lock Down Publications/The New Era Reading Group

Visit our website:
www.lockdownpublications.com

Follow us on Instagram:
Lock Down Publications

Email Us: We want to hear from you!

Prologue

Meanwhile...

The top Don of the three Italian mafia families of Philly, Don Angelo Marconi, had avoided an attempted assassination on his life by three ruffian goons who were ordered to kill him. The thwarted ambush took place in front of Antonella's Steakhouse near downtown Center City in the drizzling rain. A meeting between Don Angelo and Mickey and Hound Savage was to take place as well. But these plans too got cancelled at the moment the first shot was fired. An entire gun battle and malicious melee ensued, leaving two dead and an eternal debt owed that had to be paid. Through installments though. Don Angelo's life was saved by those he least expected. And the reality of the situation was that those who saved him didn't have to risk their own lives to save his. They could've turned and walked away. But they didn't. They chose to help, and yet, capitalize from the grudge match, and place themselves in position to benefit in the long run, once the smoke cleared and the truth was made known.

***

Three Hours After...

Johnny Mack indeed knew about the sit down that was to be between his two cousins Mickey and Hound, and Don Angelo Marconi. He himself wanted to be a part of it as well, but was told by Mickey to keep out of it due to the simple

SAVAGE FAMILY EMPIRE 2 | PRINCE A. TAUHID

facts, his name hadn't been mentioned at any time, and the mob knew nothing about him. In addition to Johnny Mack knowing about the pow-wow, he knew the location of where the restaurant sat that they were to meet. The time as well. Johnny Mack loved to burn night oil, as he had a habit of staying up late into the wee hours reading newspapers and watching news coverage on TV. He was addicted to seeking information.

A breaking news alert caught his attention on the TV screen. He'd not long turned it on, after putting away the papers and magazines. The report pertained to a failed assassination attempt on the life of a mafia leader whose name he was all too familiar with—Don Angelo Marconi. Angelo was a longtime heroin supplier to the Savage cousins. They made their living from this particular version of narcotics.

"What the fuck! I know damn well, Mickey and that fool Hound, ain't got into a shootout, with those fuckin' guineas?" he let out in soliloquy. He then snatched the phone from the hook and stabbed in the digits of Mickey's number on the keypad.

The line rang several times. Mickey finally answered.

"Mickey here."

"Mickey! What the fuck happened?! I tune in to the news on the TV, and I see something about a shootout that took place. *At Antonello's!* The steakhouse that y'all was supposed to have met with Angelo! They found two dead. One of them was in a car that was registered to Don Angelo! And the other, laid out in the middle of the street with a hole in his head!" Johnny Mack stated.

"Yeah. That's what happened. It was a wicked moment for me and Hound. But thankfully, it had nothing to do with us directly. The guineas had a beef to settle with one another. More than likely, it was another mafia family too, that aimed and gunned at Don Angelo," Mickey responded.

"Oh, okay. So that's what the situation was? It wasn't *Black Mafia,* was it?" Johnny Mack asked specifically. He knew firsthand about Hound and his gang cohorts taking off with kilos of heroin and thought maybe the Italians had found out it was Black Mafia that robbed them and struck first, with Black Mafia striking back that night. However, this wasn't the case.

"Nah. It wasn't Black Mafia. It was Italian Mafia on Italian Mafia," Mickey clarified.

"Understood. So, where the hell was y'all two at when the going got going?!"

"We was there."

"Oh, y'all was?!"

"Yeah. And if it wasn't for us, Don Angelo would be one dead son of a bitch right now! We was a God-send to him," replied Mickey.

"What!!! Hound still there with you?"

"Yeah, he's here."

"A'ight. I'm on my way over there now," Johnny Mack said and promptly hung up the phone

"A'ght, we he—"

Mickey's words were cut short when the line disconnected.

***

Once Johnny Mack made it to his cousin's pad, Mickey and Hound explained the details of all that took place. The biggest surprise to Johnny Mack of them all was that, once the shootout was over and the smoke cleared, it was Mickey and Hound who escorted Don Angelo to his place for safety. These *niggaz*, had the head man of a prominent Italian Mafia family, right there with them, all by his lonely. In a Nigga neighborhood at that! No Italian goombahs . . . no security . . . no weapons for protection . . . nothing! Just him all by himself with his black angels from heaven. Johnny Mack absolutely couldn't believe his ears when told that part.

"Humph!" Johnny Mack scoffed. "I bet that guinea muthafucka' was scared shitless, wasn't he?!" Johnny Mack asked.

"Nah. not really. He was actually grateful to us. He thanked us and everything. He hugged us and the whole nine yards. The muthafucka' talked and treated me and Hound, like we were two angels from God almighty!" Mickey stated.

"Like *Michaelangelo* and *Raphael!*" Hound remarked with a sense of wry humor.

"Fuck yeah!" Mickey punctuated with a smile and a laugh. He caused the other two to do the same.

"So how long did y'all have him here?" asked Johnny Mack.

"About an hour and some change. The Don needed to get his mind together. He was traumatized behind those bullets whizzing past that noggin of his. He took one to the shoulder though. We cleaned it and patched him up before his men made it here to get him," Hound chimed in to say.

"And who were the two that were killed?"

"The Don's driver, and one from the ops. Hound was the one who popped his ass while he was approaching and shooting at Don Angelo," Mickey related.

"Oh! Got it. So now, the Don owes you two for saving his ass?"

"Muthafuckin' right! In a major way, he owes us. And we were sure to make that clear to him, the whole time he was here," Hound stated. He was emphatic as he'd ever been.

The three cousins continued to talk throughout the night. They utilized the time to properly lay out how the groundwork was to now function to the enterprise they operated. The trio was determined to make it big in the drug business. However, one other deed had to be done before they could have the leeway to move forward how they saw fit. It was the ultimate deed. The one to be all that'll end all.

PART ONE

Chapter 1

JoJo and Winston made outstanding progress in all they had going on. She'd really begun to get into him and what he had to offer. He was introduced to her kids. They all took a trip together to the zoo and to an amusement park. The outdoor fun and sightseeing of animals was much enjoyed. This brought about a level of comfort for the kids towards him and made them feel safe and secure in the fact of knowing he was there at the house most nights, and at the a.m. hours when they awakened. Indeed, Winston had his own home, but made it his business to be there with JoJo and her kids the majority of the time.

Winston's career was that of an accountant and financial capitalist. He worked for one of the top hedge fund companies in the state at the time—Equity Financial—and drew six figure checkers in connection to the businesses that his family owned and operated. His plan was to have a home built for him and JoJo and the kids. But he also felt that there wasn't any obligation to follow through on anything, until he and JoJo were married, and she eventually bore him a baby.

JoJo had her hooks on him and her sway pinned so deep in the guy, that it never dawned on him that he was attaching himself to a female who already had five responsibilities of another man to take care of, and an option to continue in his search for some other more suitable female without a ready-made family. He could've moved on. But JoJo was the first female of color who he had the opportunity to be with sexually (before this moment in their relations, they'd had sex roughly four times) or otherwise, and he was obsessed with her and the potential of what they could achieve together. The sky was the limit.

One night, the two were situated in the bedroom of her place and having a discussion while making plans financially for the future. Winston had a few things on his mind he wanted to share and also wanted to know from her. He put a loaded question upon her.

"Josephine, I want to ask you something."

"Sure, babe. Ask me whatever you like," she responded.

"What type of future do you see us having together?"

"I honestly believe the future is bright for us, and that it holds endless possibilities. Now that I'm aware you're serious about me and my kids, based on you not walking out on us yet. I don't have any reason to fear that our future won't be a prosperous one. You provide a lot of trust and value to what we have. I've never had the opportunity to experience anything of the same before. What about you? What type of future do you see for us?"

"I feel the same as you. Except that, I'm ready for a child, sweetheart. I deserve to have a reflection of myself. And that's why I got you this, for you to think over a few things," Winston let out, then reached over to the nightstand on his side of the bed, opened the drawer to it, and brought out the gift he had for JoJo.

"What's this you have for me, Winston?" she asked with proper grammar.

JoJo had truly embraced a set of more polished and cultivated standards. There was barely anything left of her rural southern ways and speech. She'd rid herself of all those "country-ass ways" that she used to have.

Winston palmed the gift, got to his feet, and walked around the bed to get in front of JoJo. He kneeled on one knee and offered to speak once more.

"Josephine, I want to hereby ask of you to be my wife. Will you marry me?" he worded in a clear tone of voice.

JoJo had been proposed to before, by Mickey of course. But it was not to the degree that Winston took things. He'd done it the right way, in a traditional sense, and Mickey had not.

"Winston, I would absolutely love to marry you and be your wife. But first things first, I have to get a divorce from my husband and then give that power to you. In due time, I'm sure we could make this happen."

"So, you're *actually* a married woman, huh?" Winston asked. He appeared shocked to know this to be her truth.

"I am. But a lot has taken place that makes me regret the decision I made to marry him," JoJo stated.

"That's understood. But when you mentioned 'husband' before, I thought you meant like in a common law sense," Winston related what he thought.

"No. I meant my *actual* husband. But nonetheless, it shouldn't be too difficult for me to get a divorce from him. Especially not so, behind the fact of how he'd done it."

"What do you mean by that? I don't understand."

JoJo went on to explain the forgery Mickey perpetrated. She also told the story of how she and Mickey met, about her sister Natalie and his cousin Johnny Mack, and the type of life they lived. Winston began to dig deeper with his inquiries and was able to persuade JoJo to reveal more. She stopped short about nothing, other than the night they had to pack up on a whim, and head north to take refuge. JoJo told what she knew about Peaches, being she was the one between her and Mickey, and also the one she loved to hate.

"So, knowing all I do now, my next question to you would be, are you still in love with the guy?" Winston wanted to know.

"Truth is, I am. He was my first. And we have five kids together. So, I can't sit here and lie to you and say I don't love the man. However, I love you too. And as my love for him fades, the love I have for you becomes stronger." JoJo provided a classic answer.

"So, that only leaves us with one thing to do in order for you to cut ties with him and strengthen the ties that we have."

"Actually, there's two things that has to take place," informed JoJo.

"And what might the other be?"

"Indeed, I'd be willing to give you a baby, Winston. But before that could happen, I must stop taking those contraception pills I've been downing since my last baby was born, my son Isaac. My body is going to need the proper time to flush out the remaining medication from me. I didn't want any more babies at the time, because I was able to predict the direction that Mickey was headed. And it wasn't in a good space."

"Oh, okay, so that part too . . . leaving the pills alone?" Winston remarked.

"Yep."

"Then we add a baby by me to the family?"

"As many as you'd like."

"Sounds reasonable. But anyway, I bought this nice ring here for you. I want you to have it. And yes indeed, it's an engagement ring, until we're officially married," Winston said, sliding the multiple karat gift down the shaft of JoJo's ring finger, causing raw emotions to come from her in that instance.

They kissed passionately. JoJo lay back onto the bed and eased up the gown she had on and peeled her panties down both legs, taking them off. Winston was already in his sleeping clothes. He had on a plain tee shirt and a pair of briefs. His average sized manhood was now erect and bulged from behind his underwear. He wasted no more time teasing around. Winston planted his face between her legs and began to slurp on JoJo's cherry pie. He loved the flavor of her tasty treat.

While in the moment, he caused her to get off first before mounting himself atop her body and slowly penetrating her, while holding her legs high in the air. JoJo wrapped her arms around his waist as they tongue-kissed and he continued to work. Winston eventually reached a climax point and released his load into her chocolate love box. If only she'd stopped taking those birth control pills sooner, he reasoned to himself, maybe I'd have her pregnant by now. Nonetheless, they had plenty of time to perform the type of work that would get him the results he wanted.

***

Mickey made a daring getaway of the attempt that Bobby put on his freedom and his life. The cutthroat move put upon him by a former friend and former business partner, caused him to see reality for what it was now, as opposed to what he thought it to be, as the raw truth to who Bobby turned out to be, was a side to him he'd never shown before.

In his escape, Mickey found his way to the house of the mother of his two eldest children, Katherine. She lived in the Brownsville section of Miami, more commonly called "Brown-sub." Upon opening the door to let him inside, she knew then and there that something wasn't right with him. He sweated profusely, had scrapes and minor cuts about his arms, his shirt was ripped, and he looked pissed at the world and the motherfucker who created it. He'd been crossed by a longtime friend and business partner, and he didn't know what to make of the situation.

"Mickey! Are you okay?" Katherine asked. The look of disgust on his face caused concern.

"I'm good, Katherine. How you and the kids been?" he responded.

"Hey, Daddy!" Mickey's daughter came from the back and greeted him. She rushed to the living room when she heard banging on the door and his voice.

"Hey, baby. How you? Come give Daddy a hug, won't you?"

The teenager casually walked over to do so.

"Where's Elijah?" Mickey asked about his son.

"He's still out. It's not that late. And I let him hang with his friends a little while longer on the weekends. He'll be home shortly."

The day was a Friday evening.

"Oh, okay. Well look," Mickey let out and turned his head towards his daughter. "Rachel, let your momma and daddy have a word or two with each other in private, please."

"Okay, Daddy. No problem. You staying for the weekend?"

"More than likely, I will. Give me and your momma a moment, baby. Okay?" Mickey further urged. The daughter walked back to her room.

"So, what blew you through here looking the way you do?" Katherine asked.

"I made it down here yesterday afternoon. I'm on business. Ran into a problem. Had to make a break for it. Some guy tried to rob me," Mickey stated.

Katherine continued to look upon him and shake her head.

"More street business?" she asked.

"For the most part." He kept his lie going.

Katherine continued to shake her head at him. "You just don't plan on changing anytime soon, do you, Mickey Savage? Lord knows you're just as reluctant to doing the right thing as you wanna be, ain't you? Hardheaded as ever. That makes it more difficult to change. Because you're too stuck in your ways."

"I am who I am, Kat. And I'mma be who I'mma be. I'll never change. This is me every day. Hate me or love me. But only God can judge me," Mickey stated.

"I'm not condemning you, Methuselah Savage. I'd like for you to finally realize that you got *seven* kids, man. And if it's possible, a better example for your boys would be a good thing. You got four. Please keep this in mind moving forward."

"I will, Katherine. I will. Now, can I use your phone please? I need to make a really important call."

"Sure. Go ahead," Katherine said, pointing at the location where the phone sat. "Go right on."

Mickey contacted the hotel where he'd made his daring escape. He requested the room where Sparkle was still situated. She had no knowledge of what transpired.

"Hello!" she answered.

"Sparkle, it's me, Daddy. Look, don't ask any questions and don't give me a hard time. All I need is you to do is, what I tell you to, and I'll explain later," Mickey stated.

"Okay, Daddy. I'm listening."

"Pack all of our bags and get the hell out the hotel suite. Catch a cab to the train station and take the train back to Philadelphia and go to my place. Stay put until I get home. I'll be there either Monday or Tuesday. Do you understand me on this?"

"I do."

"Good. Talk later," he concluded and hung up the phone. He made his way to the kitchen where Katherine was at that point.

The two began to talk over cups of coffee and slices of pie. They related how life was for them and about the things that had taken place throughout the time. Mickey mentioned about the separation he and JoJo were going through, and that they'd both decided it was best to go about things the way they were. Katherine made him aware that she had a male friend in her life now, and that the two had plans to go into business together.

Katherine was happily situated in the relationship she was now involved in but held a special space in her heart for Mickey. If only he would change and do the right thing. It would certainly look better on him in the eyes of the kids if he'd done so.

"Mickey, it won't be too much longer before the kids graduate high school and wanna go off to college. What do you intend to do about helping to pay for their education? I'm hoping you putting money away to help pay college tuition. They're getting older by the day, you know. And also, my friend, Glen, has offered to take care of everything. But he's not their father. You are—and it's your responsibility. Not his. I just need to know from you what to expect in the future regarding this?"

Katherine took Mickey down the path of a conversation that was long overdue for them. She'd been patient and considerate long enough. And now, the wait was over.

Rachel went unnoticed by her parents as she stood in the hallway close to the kitchen where they sat and listened in on all that they talked about. She loved her father and missed him dearly. However, there was a need for him to prove to her and her brother that he loved and missed them as well, in the same way that Glen had, if not more. Rachel didn't know anything about Glen offering to pay their way through college. That one was a newbie to her. And with the knowledge of it now, it caused her to have an elevated level of respect for him and placed pressure on her father to perform better at being a father in her eyes. If Mickey failed to do so, he would run the risk of her transferring all of her love for him, over to the one who deserved it most, with that being Glen, the man who showed and proved the most that he cared.

"I got a plan in place, Kat. I do. I been thinking of this very same thing here for the longest. And I know at all costs, I got to deliver. When I get back to Philadelphia, I plan to open a trust account in the kids' names and begin putting money into it monthly."

"Beginning with my two first, I assume?" Katherine wanted assurance.

"Of course, that. They'll be on their way before the kids by JoJo would. I've got more time to prepare with them. But nonetheless, I'mma be sure to put at least twenty thousand or more towards their trust account in the next month or so," Mickey said, revealing his intentions.

"Well, on another note. How soon will it be before they are able to come and spend some time with you and . . . *'whoever'* it is you got in your life now? I need a break! They ain't never had the chance to stay with you. Maybe this summer will be a good time to start. What you say?"

"I don't have a problem with that, Katherine. Not at all. But, please. Allow me the time to clean up some of the mess that's going on in my world. Then, Rachel and Elijah can come enjoy time with their pop."

"I hear you. And you really do need to clean up your act, Mickey. You're too smart of a man and getting too old to continue on like this. Get yourself together, please. That's all we need for you to do, okay?" Katherine encouraged. "And yes, you can stay the night. But you already know we can't sleep in the same bed. You can have the couch. And again, your boy should be home soon. He needs a talking to. By his daddy! Although you showed up in an awkward way, your timing was perfect," she said further, with a smile.

Mickey chuckled at her remarks.

***

His stay in Miami was for the remainder of the weekend. He then took the train back to Philly the following Monday. Katherine and his two oldest gave him a world of a lot to think over, as they pleaded with the most stubborn man they knew, to change his ways and do better. At least for them and the five others he had to take care of. May God forbid his boys to make the choices and decisions in life as he had and prevent them from being the type of man that he was. Only time would tell.

Chapter 2

Hound was sure to do his duty and gave Frank and Lacy their share of the loot they'd jacked the mob out of. They were both given twenty kilos each, twenty thousand in cash, and a pistol, leaving Hound with all that was to be left over once he paid Neil the ten kilos he was owed for the tip on the stash house. Neil and Hound met up to have a conversation about it all.

"I see everything worked out in your favor, big guy," Neil initiated, referring to the six-five frame of Hound and the two hundred sixty-eight pounds he weighs.

"Yes indeed. Just like a wise politician telling lies to his strongest supporters. It worked. Things paid off well in the end. But, to tell you the truth, Neil, at first, I thought you were bullshittin' me. And then, the more eager you got to have someone pull it off and by you going along with me to show the location where Peter lived, I knew then it was the real deal. It also helped out by me already knowing who the old fuck was. I had seen him a time or two in the past. But, I wanna ask you this," Hound said.

"What's that, Hound?"

"By you knowing Pete was holding like that, why didn't you take on the mission yourself? To go in and do the damn thing?" Hound wanted to know. "I'm just asking because I'm curious, that's all."

Hound dug in deep with his question because he felt the need to know what Neil's true intent might've been. He continued on before Neil had the opportunity to respond. "I know that the Marconi family and the Scalia bunch, have been hard at each other's necks for a period of time now. And it seems to me with you being a Scalia associate, that you will be doing them a favor by helping harm the Marconi's any type of way, so as to become a made man. So why not have you pulled the caper by yourself?"

"It's because, Hound, had I done so, you wouldn't have all that you now do, and you wouldn't be in the current position where you stand," Neil stated in a humorous way, causing the both of them to laugh out loud. "Also, Hound, by you being a Black guy doing the deed, blows more dust into their eyes to keep them from seeing the picture more clearly on what's happening to them. They'll never know who done it. Had other Italians done so, the Marconi phonies could narrow things down. Ain't too many places in Philly an Italian can sell 'H', you know. But, the Black smack dealer, he has many places to work. You get my point?"

"Now I do, since you put it that way," responded Hound.

"And these ten keys I got are gonna be sold out in Pittsburgh and in Ohio, not here in Philly."

"Smart man, Neil, smart man."

"And I need for you to be that too. Lay low for a while before you begin moving what you got, you know. In order to give the city time to adjust to the shortage of supply that's to occur and finally replenish once again. Then, once that takes place, ease the product you're holding onto, into the fray. No one'll know a fucking thing at that point."

"Got you, Neil. And you take care, you hear? I'll see you around. And hopefully, we can do more good work together in the future to come," Hound stated as he greeted Neil away.

Hound pulled off in the new Cadillac he recently bought with the money taken from Peter's home. He was now styling and profiling.

Although he was eager as all hell to take those kilos of heroin he had, break them down, and redistribute them to the streets, Hound knew that the advice Neil laid on him was the best words to follow, as it made all the sense in the world to do so. And another thing, he knew he had to ensure that Frank and Lacy had the same outlook on how to go about doing things as he and Neil. If any mishap was to occur and word had gotten out on what they'd done, the consequences could be severe. Not only had they invaded a home, taken people hostage, and robbed the mob, they caused the death of a person who was dear to the others. Not to mention what was done to the family pet.

Hound and crew had no knowledge on whether the particular mob band they'd violated had any ties to the police or FBI agents. For sure, they did. Additional problems were created in that regard. Sylvia's sister, who died during the stick-up, had a son who was a lieutenant on the police force, and he would stop at nothing until the crime was solved by vigilante justice or courtroom justice. Therefore, they had to move carefully.

***

Once Mickey finally made it back to Philly, he knew how important it was to have a conversation with Johnny Mack about all that happened down in Miami at the hotel.

"Johnny Mack! We may got more problems on our hands about that Georgia thing than we originally thought," Mickey stated in a voice of anxiety.

"How so?" Johnny Mack responded.

"Kavanaugh, man! That muthafucka' turned on me! The son of a bitch drew down on me and Miss Peaches. He tried to arrest me and take me in. The bastard shot at me too. And actually did put a bullet in Peaches. I'm sure he intended to kill her and the baby she's carrying. Now that the truth of the rape and murder of that while girl done finally came out. I showed you the newspapers that covered the story. It was his goddamn nephew the one responsible. The sick fuck killed himself before they had the opportunity to arrest him," Mickey stated.

Johnny Mack looked at him and shook his head.

"Now you see why I warned you back then not to say shit to that cutthroat muthafucka' about the incident that took place in your house?! That bastard would've been snaked us had you done so!" Johnny Mack was sure to remind Mickey of what he said to him the same night they concealed the bodies of those two cops who were killed.

"Shit! I'm glad I did take heed to your warning. It protected us in the long run."

"And you had the nerve to think you was actually doing something by having that Peaches girl continue to put the pussy on him, become pregnant, and attempt to use that as a tool to blackmail that fucker with, huh. In the end, all he done was try to X you out, and murder her and the seed of his she carry. The man ain't got no soul, Mickey. That muthafucka' ain't shit, you hear me what I say! Hopefully, Peaches and that baby is okay," Johnny Mack let out.

"Peaches is doing fine. The bullet she took went to the shoulder. Not to the belly—nothing life threatening. I had my other girl Sparkle check into things and find out the situation."

"So, what they plan on doing with Peaches?" asked Johnny Mack.

"The dirty bastard, Bobby, had the D.A. in Miami, fix her bail sky-high to keep her from getting out. He's trying to punish her," Mickey related.

"Bail! Sky-high! Hell, on what charge?! She ain't committed no crime."

"They trumped up some bogus bullshit on the girl. Bobby is making it his business to do her wrong. But I strongly believe me and Miss Peaches will eventually have the last laugh on that. In due time," Mickey lastly stated on the subject.

"So long as the muthafucka' ain't got shit to pin on us, we shouldn't have a thing to worry about. But to move forward, I held down the fort while you were gone. And, I got Natalie straight too. So, you ain't got to worry about her having nothing more to do with you and JoJo's business. Everything is kosher now," Johnny Mack said.

"And what about Hound? Our security?"

"Everything good on that end too. Although he do seem to be really deep into that Black Mafia business now-a-days, then into how *we* run things. You know how Hound is. Maybe this could turn out good for all of us. But at all costs, he's family. Not like you and I with our laid-back personality. Hound got a serious appetite for action. The raw kind. And we more low profile."

"Yeah, I know. He's good though. He has the leeway to do whatever it is he chooses to. So long as the type of action he's got an appetite for, don't bring problems our way," Mickey iterated his thoughts on Hound being a family member and establishing his legacy in the other circle he helped run.

"And about the product. We were already low. But got really low while you were in Florida. You got anything put to the side for hard times?" asked Johnny Mack.

"I got a little something. But not hardly enough. More than likely, I gotta go see Angelo at some point soon. Be sure to get the money to me y'all brought in by the time we meet up tomorrow. All of us need to talk. At four in the afternoon. I'll set up a meeting with the supply man for more product after we come together on a plan."

"Sounds good by me. And in the meantime, don't worry yourself too much about those two pigs we put away back then. Me, personally, I can always do something you should've did long ago. Hire a gun to put the threat away for good. I know a few people. And they're good at what they do," said Johnny Mack.

"We may have to go that route at some point in the future. But Bobby is a powerful man now. Much more than he was back then."

"A threat is a threat, Mickey. No matter a powerful man or a peon. But hey, let me know, okay? I'm gone," Johnny Mack lastly said then left his cousin to be to himself.

Mickey had a lot to think over and serious problems to eliminate.

Chapter 3

One Day Later ...

Mickey contacted the Italian supplier for more product. Angelo told him that the earliest they could do another deal would be that coming Friday. It was only Wednesday. The numbers needed to be discussed first, then all else would be mulled over afterwards. Mickey was okay in knowing that much. So long as Angelo still had product to sell.

Later in the day, Mickey and Johnny Mack came together as planned. They weren't able to get in touch with Hound. He was off in Atlantic City enjoying himself. He and an old female friend he'd reconnected with. It was the lovely Shug Tatum. They couldn't get enough of one another, as it had been years since they last spent time together. Thankfully, Shug's contact to her mother's home hadn't changed when Hound made the call. His excuse to her for why he reached out was that he was doing better in life now than he was before, and that he didn't want to reach out to her until he was in a position to do something nice for her for a change. The truth behind it all was that certain types of women have their own special type of way, with how they make a man feel when they do all that they do. It was Shug who had this special effect on Hound, as only her love making could do. And at the same time, he had his effect on her. It worked both ways with those two.

Unbeknownst to Hound, Shug was already in the area where he was. She was in New York City working out the final stage of negotiations in a record deal she'd struck. Her mother contacted her in the hotel suite she stayed in and provided the phone number Hound left. Shug immediately contacted him from there. They got busy with sexual action the very moment they met up in AC at the suite Hound booked. They experienced magical moments every time they shared intimacy together.

***

The Friday Mickey anticipated was upon him. Angelo had him meet at a different location than before. In South Philly indeed, but at a cheese shop owned by Angelo. He had a space in the back of the place he'd made an office out of. Something was different with this particular meeting than the times of the past. Angelo now had more security on hand. There appeared to be a trust issue of some sort. Johnny Mack was brought along as always. He and Mickey both took heed of what played out before their eyes with the added security men.

Mickey was put through the process of being checked for weapons prior to entry into the room where the Don of his family was situated. He understood that whatsoever it was going on, it wasn't personal, only business.

I wonder what the fuck done took place to make Angelo up his security? Ain't no telling. Knowing the history of these bastards the way that I do, they probably at war again with another mafia family. Oh well. Maybe he'll let me know what's up. Maybe he won't, Mickey thought.

Once granted access into the room with Angelo, the two shook hands and began to discuss business.

"Mickey," he called out his name with a hoarse voice. "I'm glad to see you made it safely with your money," Angelo said.

25

"Yeah. I'm here. Had no problems in traffic or with the police. But I got a question, Don Angelo," Mickey responded.

"And what's that?"

"What's the reason for the extra security? The extra frisking when we arrived? I would have thought that you and I are past that point now in business," Mickey questioned.

"We are, Mickey. Something happened I can't speak with you on. It wasn't anything on your behalf. But I'm trying to get down to the bottom of it. And the way I'm going about it is best to keep a safeguard on me and my family." Don Angelo provided enough of an explanation to keep Mickey from feeling as though blame was put upon him.

"That's understandable. But anyway, I've got about five hundred thousand to spend with you on product. I'm really low and need supply to satisfy the demand of my customer base," Mickey said to him.

"I'm afraid I have some not so good news for you, Mickey."

"I don't understand, Don."

"My business for the product you looking to buy, is temporarily put on hold," stated Angelo.

Mickey jarred his head at the words of the Don.

"What's the issue, Don Angelo?"

"Again, something happened. And it's not proper for me to speak with you on it. I have to put my business on hold for the time being, to help me figure out all I need to know. That's all I can tell you."

"So, this half-million in cash I got here don't mean me any good to you?"

"Not at this particular time, it don't," Don Angelo stated emphatically.

"And when might I be able to spend this money with you?" Mickey stated, patting the side of the leather tote bag he carried the cash in.

"I'll be sure to have you notified when I'm ready."

"Not a problem, Don Angelo," Mickey responded, then stood to his feet to leave. "You take care and have a nice remainder of your day."

Don Angelo nodded his head at the words of Mickey in response to wish him well also. He continued to hold his seat at the table and drank on his cup of espresso. The time was 12:00 p.m., lunch hour.

***

Mickey and Johnny Mack exited the cheese shop and got back into the car with the money they'd arrived with. He had a very disappointing look on his face. Johnny Mack took notice of both the look on Mickey's face, and the bag of money instead of heroin product. This only meant one thing, no deal was made.

But why? Johnny Mack silently questioned.

"Mickey!" Johnny Mack called out his name in disbelief as he fired up the car. He looked upon Mickey with his mouth held wide.

"What the hell!"

"Angelo says that his business with the 'H' is on hold for right now. That something happened he couldn't speak with me about," Mickey explained.

"Something happened, my ass! I got bills to pay and other shit to do! And what we 'spose to do in the meantime?" Johnny Mack stated angrily.

"We ain't got no choice but to wait."

"The hell we do! Or we can go out and find a new supplier. I need to get my hands on some goddamn dope! My livelihood depends on it! No dope means no money! And we can't have that!"

"My livelihood depends on it too, Johnny Mack. And I got shit to do as well. But I'm willing to wait until Angelo opens the door for business again."

"And you a goddamn fool, to sit your ass around and wait for a fuckin' guinea, to make a decision on when he feels like he wanna sell you his dope! Ain't no way! Not me! That muthafucka' done lost his mind, Mickey! I'mma go out and find somebody else to deal with. That's all there is to it," declared Johnny Mack.

"You free to do what you wanna do. I'll put your money back in your hands when we get to the house. But I'm telling you, that won't be a wise thing to do, to break rank, and shop outside of who we normally deal with," Mickey cautioned.

"Well, leave me to find that out on my own. Because no matter what, something gotta give. And the bill collectors don't accept excuses as payment."

Mickey shrugged his shoulders and turned his head sideways behind Johnny Mack's remarks. He had no intent to try and stop him from doing what his mind was made up to do. Business was business no matter what. And Johnny Mack had the option to go on about it, however he saw fit. He was his own man.

Chapter 4

The streets of Philly began to dry up of the heroin supply that was once plentiful. No one had any real weight to sell. Only a limited amount was being sold in baggies on retail. Hound, Frank, and Lacy held tightly to the material that they'd hit for, and the agreement to not sell anything for a time being, was being followed. That was, until Lacy took it upon himself to break rank, and began pumping the portion that he had of the take, to the dealers and junkies who lurk on his side of town in west Philly. They were looking to kill or die to get a fix, or their hands on something to sell.

At the time, Lacy had only family members of his that he put on. They sold his product and protected him. The money poured in seemingly. Only twenty-dollar and fifty-dollar bags were sold. He and his people took ten kilos and flooded the blocks.

On the other hand, Hound lived and operated in the north Philly section of the city. In an area that was referred to as the "Badlands," he'd heard through the grapevine about the business Lacy had going on in his hood and decided to take a trip across the Schuylkill River to Lacy's territory, to have a look at how things functioned and to talk with his homie. Hound knew where Lacy's mother lived, and knew that if anything, he'd be there attending to her, and spending some of his new money on her and her home.

The day was Sunday. Hound parked down the street from the house and approached on foot. He noticed three aggressive looking dudes situated on the porch. He instantly knew that they had to be body-men on hand, toting pistols for Lacy.

This nigga got airtight security and everything out this bitch, don't he! Hound thought.

He walked closer to the porch. It was elevated off the ground on a concrete flooring. About six feet in height.

"Yeah! Who you looking for?" one of the dudes hollered out at Hound. He positioned himself in a way like he was ready to draw a pistol on Hound, with any false move he made.

None of the three had any idea that Hound was a friend of Lacy's.

"Be easy, gangsta!" Hound offered a quick response. "I ain't here for problems. I'm here to see a partner of mine, Lacy. This his mom's place, right? Mrs. Hightower, right?" He provided a specific name.

"It could be. It could be not. But the real question is, who you, nigga?!" asked the apparent leader of the three.

"Look bro, if Lacy in there, tell him it's me, Hound."

"The top guy gave a heads up to one of the other two for him to go inside and make Lacy aware of the person who was there to see him. Shortly thereafter, Lacy finally appeared at the front door to find out exactly that it was Hound there to see him.

"Lacy! What's happening, my guy! And will you please tell these cats who I be," Hound stated.

"What's good, Hound," responded Lacy. "And 'these cats' you see here, is my family. Just like you, Mickey, and Johnny Mack. They only doing what I pay them to do. And doing their duty to family like they supposed to do. They good," Lacy made his street friend aware. "Y'all stand down. He good. But do your duty when I let him come up," he further said to them in a low voice out of Hound's hearing.

"Is it safe to come up now or what, my nigga?" asked the tall and husky Hound.

"Yeah, you good. Come on up. But don't take things personal. It's only business," Lacy said to Hound, giving word to approach.

Hound began to walk up the steps. "Don't take what personal?"

When he reached the porch, all three of Lacy's bodyguards drew down on Hound with their pistols. He threw his hands up in surrender. They then proceeded to pat him from neck to feet for weapons.

"This part," Lacy proclaimed. "Don't take this personal."

"Well, goddamn, Lacy! It's like this now!" Hound let out in disbelief. He began to get pissed at Lacy now, in addition to already being so behind what he'd heard Lacy had going on.

"Damn right it is, nigga!" The lead body man said with a snarl. "And the fact of the matter is, we don't know you! It's our job to perform like this. Just as Lacy said already. It ain't personal. Only business," the guy further spat, taking the automatic pistol Hound carried on a temporary basis. The pocketknife as well.

"It's all good, dude, it's all good," responded Hound to the pat-search. He continued throughout, to look on at Lacy in disbelief. There was a cold stare of vitriol in his eyes towards Lacy.

Hound was then escorted into the house. He and Lacy stepped into the back room for privacy. Lacy initiated the talk at that point.

"How the hell you know to find me here, Hound?" he asked.

"You might be new money, Lacy. But you still got old ways. But the real question I got for you is, why the hell you go against the agreement in place to not sell any of the dope for a time being?" That's what I'm trying to know," Hound vented at Lacy in a way.

"The last I checked, Hound, I'm a grown ass man, my nigga! And I don't need nobody trying to dictate to me when and how to do shit!" He returned fire to match that of his visitor. "And besides, it was too much muthafuckin' money to be had! And it wasn't no need to keep sittin' on that shit, only for the cops to come knock me off with it! Or for some other muthafucka' to come jack me for it! And speaking on jacking for product, don't you still got that list of stash houses inside that address book that can stand a robbing right now? I got a few die-hard young cousins who looking to do work to become what we are. But on top of that . . . fuck them guinea cheese eating Italian bastards! Nigga, *Black Mafia* run Philly now! You know that. Or you must'a forgot! And what they supposed to do anyway? You see these killers I got 'round me now. *I'm* the one with the juice. *I'm* that nigga! And *I'm* the only nigga in the city who got product for sell. Ya hear! And it feels good to be that," Lacy boasted to Hound in his face. He was long winded with what he had to say.

Hound had nothing to rebut with. He just looked at Lacy and let him talk his shit. However, he was taken aback by Lacy's choice of words and behavior. He knew it could lead to both of them being killed if he didn't get a hand on it.

"Bad move by you, bro. Really bad move," Hound finally responded. "The shit you doing could potentially spark a war with those cats, if word got back to them who it was to rob their spot," he cautioned, something he found himself doing a lot of with Lacy of late. Something he usually wouldn't do. This wasn't a good thing in his view. Retribution needed to be exacted, and that was all there was to it.

"If you ain't heard or noticed by now, Hound, I'm built for war, my nigga," Lacy replied with an even more cocky attitude. Hound simply shook his head yet again.

Hound had a thought. *A hard head makes a soft ass each and every time.*

He turned away from Lacy and began to make an exit out of the room towards the front door. Lacy lagged behind, making his way back to the den area where he was previously situated. He'd been busy watching a baseball game.

Hound suddenly turned to face Lacy once more before he disappeared. He had a few last words to say.

"So, you insist on things going this way between us, Lacy? Again, it's not good, no type of way to be getting off the product right now. It's only gonna draw attention. The kind we don't need."

Lacy took a serious look at Hound, as if to ask, *is this nigga crazy, or don't understand English that good!*

He made it his duty to respond to Hound in a way to indicate to him he meant business. "It's a bit too late to stop a moving train, now ain't it? And everything you just said may apply to you and how you intend to move. But not to me, homie. I'm my own boss. With my own team. And again, it ain't nothing personal. It's strictly business, fam. Strictly business. So you be good now, you hear," Lacy stated, then disappeared.

The lead body-man opened the front door for Hound to leave. Once on the porch again, the door closed and was locked. Hound was then given back his gun and knife. He walked down the steps and away towards his car to go back to his territory.

A beef between him and Lacy was born on that particular day. Hound became determined to deal with any and all forms of disrespect that Lacy perpetrated against him. He felt betrayed in the aftermath of the robbery to secure Lacy with the drugs and money he now had. It was Hound who brought him in. and now it would have to be Hound to take him out. A decision was made then and there by Hound: Kill Lacy!

Chapter 5

One Week Later...

Mickey finally was able to get in touch with Hound. There was an urgent issue that needed to be discussed, and he told Hound he wanted to talk, to stop by his place at the first opportunity he got.

Hound answered the call his cousin made and headed to see him to know what he had on his mind he wanted to talk about.

The thing Mickey wanted to talk about was already predicted by Hound. He knew that the spots the three of them operated had no product for sale, and that more than likely, Mickey had caught wind of how business was going on the west side of the Schuylkill River, over in Lacy's area, and wanted to talk about that. Mickey didn't know too many people in west Philly, let alone other heroin dealers. But he'd heard a name though. A guy by the name, "Black Mafia Lacy," and knew Hound had stronger ties to these dudes than he did. He wanted to see what Hound knew.

"I'm here, Mickey. What's on your mind these days? And I'm already knowing that it ain't no work right now. The city has dried up. There's plenty of money to be made, but no dope to make it with," Hound stated upon being let inside.

"And that's what I wanna speak with you about. Because you been around here longer than me and Johnny Mack, and you know more people than we do," responded Mickey.

"And you wanna know what from me?"

"Two things. Who the fuck is 'Black Mafia Lacy?' And if you know him, how can we get with him about business? You're more familiar with them dudes than me, and you can point us in the right direction."

"Well, I ain't gonna lie to you and say I don't know who he is when I do. But I can't put you in touch with dude though. Me and that nigga had some words and fell out not long ago," Hound explained.

"Oh really!"

"Fuck yeah! The nigga had the balls to try and talk real greasy to me in front of his people. They were supposed to be his bodyguards and toting the pistol for dude. But it's gonna be me who has the last say on how this is to go between us," Hound declared.

"Well, I-be-damned! Didn't know that. But, word is, he's the nigga who got control over a few junkie-caves that's doing wonderful out in west. And he might be the only muthafucka' in all of Philly, who got H for sale. And I'm hot about that! Because I'm not able to get some of the money I know him and his squad making. And my hunger for the almighty dollar on shark mode right about now! I gotta have it! So, is it any way you can put the business to the front, and the beef between you two behind you? I'm only asking, Hound."

Hound looked at Mickey with a blank expression. He took a long pause between Mickey's words and offered a response.

"Mickey. Listen to how that shit may sound to me. You already know, once you're my enemy, ain't no going back to normal from there. It is what it is. And the only way I can see myself doing that is to not be in position to do so. Because that's what it's gonna be. I'mma put that nigga in the dirt! Or he's gonna do it to me if I don't get to him first!" Hound spat. War was declared with him and Lacy.

"Oh shit! It's that bad?" Mickey retorted.

"Hell yeah! Shit is that bad, fam! And it ain't no fixing it."

"Well, I need to get my hands on some work to sell. And you my family. So that means, you need to do so as well. Now what we gonna do about meeting the demand?"

"What happened to you getting our supply from Angelo?"

"Fuck that guinea piece of shit! I went to the bastard with a half-million dollars, and he had the nerve to turn me around with it." Johnny Mack felt some type of way about that. "But I guess they back on their racist shit again and not fucking with no one but the Italians. The blacks must be blackballed in the underworld from doing business with them. They holding onto all the product for themselves," Mickey stated. This was his theory at least.

Hound shook his head behind Mickey's words.

"It don't surprise me at all that those muthafucka's' would all of a sudden cut you out the loop like that. How do they come to the conclusion that the black dope pusher is now a threat to them in any type of way, and they the ones having the shit shipped in, besides all the racketeering and other shit they got going on in their world," Hound responded.

"Beats me, fam. But Angelo is not really the one to deny me like that. He claimed something happened, but didn't say what. So, fuck it! I just gotta find somebody else that a half-million dollars might mean something to. Even if I have to take a trip to Harlem, New York. I hear there's some high-profile nigga up there by the name 'Bumpy Johnson.' And he's specifically looking for other black dealers to do business with. Something about him trying to establish 'Ten Harlems' outside the real one. Whatever that supposed to mean."

Hound took another long pause to absorb all Mickey had to say. There was no way in all America that he had thirty kilos of pure H, and his cousin had that much money to spend on this particular product, and he didn't serve him from the batch he was sitting on. The offer was too good to pass up.

"Let me ask you something, Mickey."

"Talk to me."

"How many kilos of 'Horse' would you normally get for the type of money you tryna spend?" asked Hound.

Mickey furrowed his eyebrows and jarred his head at the question.

"What the hell do it matter for, nigga, if you ain't got shit to sell me, or don't know anybody to do so either?" Mickey responded in a typical fashion like Hound would expect.

"Nigga! How the hell you know what I got or who I know?! I was given the name 'Hound' for a reason. That's because I always had instincts to hunt shit down or lead someone on the trail where something was located."

"Okay. Since you wanna play it like that, I usually get a kilo of H for twenty-five thousand a pop. So, for a half-million with Angelo, that'll get me twenty, plus an additional three as a cap for doing good business. Now, your turn. Who you know or what you got?" Mickey let out. He was very eager to hear what Hound now had to say.

Hound stared at Mickey oddly. He was contemplating making a decision on whether it was okay at that point, to reveal a thing or two, or simply continue to keep quiet. If anything, he knew Mickey was family, and that he was one of those who had his best interest at heart. Hound had a duty to not let his people down, and to eventually make Mickey aware of what the deal was. However, this was to take a little more time before he could. He made up an excuse.

"Look, give me until the weekend to come up with something. I'll be sure to make a way for you to get what you looking for. Can we agree to that?" Hound asked.

"No problem. Do what you do, fam. Just get me some product for us to sell."

"And that, I shall do. You have my word. If you don't take matters into your own hands first and go out and find somebody. I know how impatient you can get."

Mickey still had his mind stayed on finding out who this 'Black Mafia Lacy' cat was, so to at least have a conversation with him, and possibly negotiate a future deal.

Chapter 6

Mickey knew just who to go to about who it was he wanted to know about. There was a dude in the streets he was familiar with that knew some of everybody. His name was Fredrick Owens, aka "Streetlife." He was a dope head who shot heroin to get high. It was his preferred drug of choice. Nonetheless, he had control over his habit and only shot the best grade of narcotics into his veins. He had a level of standards to how he did things, and didn't carry himself like any ol' junkie. And at that particular time, Lacy and crew had the best around, not to mention being the only ones with anything to sell. And Lacy never cut the product. He sold it as is, the way that it was.

Roughly an hour after having a talk with Hound, Mickey hit the streets to go out and find Streetlife. He knew where he lived and also where the guy hung out at, over in the Kensington neighborhood of Philly. Streetlife was a pool-shark. He had a raw talent when it came to pushing a stick. The main spot, Streetlife's Parlor, wasn't too far from the small house Mickey owned. This was the first place he decided to look.

"I got a hundred bucks over here on Streetlife," Mickey announced to all would-be betters. He located who he was looking for, then put a bet on his skills. It was a new game. He caused heads to look in the direction he sat.

"I'll call it, and I wanna raise that bet to two hundred," said another old-school hustler who looked on.

"You ain't said nothing but a word, my guy. And this not poker. I'm not gonna fold. We can up the bet too. Now I got 'four hundred' on Streetlife. Because I believe in him that much," Mickey responded.

"Bet it! Because I believe in my homie Buck that much. I know he's the God-honest truth, in my opinion."

"An opinion is just like an asshole, everybody has one. And if you believe in your guy as much as you claim to, let's just make it a grand then, what about that? Because I trust in Streetlife," stated Mickey.

"I ain't got a grand. Eight hundred all I can do, big timer," the old hustler responded.

"It's a bet! And we got a great pool match on our hands, fellas!" Mickey let out loud enough for everyone to hear. The game began at that point.

The battle was intense between Streetlife and the other guy. Nonetheless, it was Streetlife to outperform the competition and get the W over the L. He put smiles on the faces of everybody who bet on him. Mickey topped the list.

Streetlife barely knew of Mickey but came to the knowledge that he was being looked for by him, a cat who had plenty of paper on hand, and a lot of business about himself. He knew the benefit of having a friend like Mickey and what all he may be able to make happen. He viewed a partnership with Mickey the same as the world viewed a friendship with Jesus. "Oh what a friend they have in him." However, he had to know what the stranger wanted with him.

Mickey made his approach. The two men stood tall and looked one another in the eyes. They shared a smile behind the victory Streetlife claimed. The thought was to know, who was the guy that was willing to put up a thousand-dollar bet on his pool-shooting skills? They may have more in common that meets the eye.

"Streetlife!" Mickey calls him out by name over the music playing from the jukebox.

"The one and only. And who might you be?" he responded. "I've seen you around a time or so, but don't know who you are."

"I'm Mickey Savage, my brother. You probably know my people more than you know me."

"And they call your people by what name now?"

"He goes by Hound Savage. Or either Big Hound."

"Oh, yeah-yeah-yeah! Big Hound. The nigga who bought all that expensive shit for females me and my guys scored for. He brought me to you too for you to buy some of what we had," Streetlife recalled.

"Exactly!" replied Mickey. "That be the both of us."

The two shook hands.

"So, what brought you here? It's obvious you looking for me," Streetlife stated.

"Well, for one, I knew the place where you mainly push your stick. And, I also wanted to rap with you about a thing or two."

"Oh! You do? Well, as you may know, in today's world, information does come with a price tag," Streetlife stated in a confident manner. It was apparent Mickey came to him for something, so he figured he may as well make a profit off it while he had the advantage.

"Like always, I'm prepared to pay for what it is I want."

Mickey then counted out three hundred-dollar bills and offered them to Streetlife. He gladly accepted.

"So, what you tryna find out, Mickey Savage?"

Mickey leaned closer to whisper what it was he had to say. He wanted to keep his words strictly business between them.

"I've got serious money I'm tryna spend for weight in it. The only somebody that I've heard of who may got that type of quantity and product, is some cat out in west Philly named 'Black Mafia Lacy!' You know anything about him?"

"Maybe I do. Maybe I don't. Who's to say? And it also depends on what you mean about some 'serious paper?' And what I get out the deal for who I know. I got an itch that needs to be scratched every now and then. So, if you know of me, then you know of that too," said Streetlife to Mickey's inquiry.

"I'm aware of who you be and what you do. But back to the point at hand. I got between fifty and seventy-five thousand, depending, that I wanna put towards buying supply. And if you're able to set up a meeting between me and that cat Lacy, I'll see to it that a thousand dollars' worth of product is put in your hands. Only, if a deal happens. Now, how soon can you do what you do and make this happen?"

The time was still early and the night young. There was enough time for Streetlife to make a run out west to see Lacy and set up a meeting for Mickey. He looked at him to properly gauge his energy. It was quickly made known that Mickey was for real, that he needed shit to sell. And now.

"I might be able to make the meeting happen tonight before eleven. So why don't we hop in your car and head on over to west Philly, shall we? And I strongly advise that you take off all that jewelry you got on there. It's too many goddamn stick-up niggaz that live over that way!" responded Streetlife with a word of caution added into the mix.

Mickey peeled off two more hundred-dollar bills and passed them to Streetlife. The two got into the Ford Mustang GT Mickey recently bought and made the drive to the other side of town.

Chapter 7

Throughout the ride, Mickey had proper time to chop it up thoroughly with Streetlife like he wanted to. Turned out, dude knew Lacy far more than he originally let on he had. Lacy once dated a female cousin of his.

Streetlife knew where the bar was Lacy had recently bought or probably muscled somebody out of. He'd visited in the days leading up to the day. Lacy now utilized the place as a hang out spot slash office to conduct business. There were a couple of pool tables inside the place. If for whatever reason Lacy wasn't there when they arrived, Streetlife could shoot a few rounds for a couple of dollars, until the person running the place contacted Lacy, and he made it to see who was there to see him, and why.

When they made it to the bar, Lacy wasn't there. He finally arrived roughly forty-five minutes after the fact. He went to his office space in the back and had his bodyguards frisk Mickey and Streetlife thoroughly before they were to be allowed in his presence. It was the same three guys who searched Hound the day he went to see Lacy.

Upon entering, Streetlife went to work with his gift of gab. "Lacy-Lacy-Lacy! How you been, my nigga! You looking good too, boy. Sharp as the blade on a surgeon's scalpel."

"I'm doing good, Street. I can't complain. What the business be though? Let's get straight to that part. And who you brought with you to see me?" Lacy responded. He turned his head slightly to look at Mickey at that point.

"No doubt. Let's get straight to that part. I got this guy here with me," he pointed at Mickey, "who looking to do big business, if the product right."

"I'm Mickey Savage." The two shook hands.

"My product always right. And big business like what?"

"Big business like a hundred grand big business," stated Mickey. "And I know you don't know me like that, but Streetlife here do. He and my people pretty tight. You may or may not know who my people is. I don't know."

Mickey already had knowledge that Lacy and Hound knew one another. Hound had already revealed this. But, because of the beef the two had going on, Mickey didn't want to readily mention Hound's name, and potentially ruin a business deal he was in the middle of trying to put together.

"Why do I detect a southern accent to your voice?" Lacy asked.

"I'm originally from down south. Georgia be my home state. PA now," replied Mickey.

"Oh, okay. That explains. But who your people you are referring to?"

"Big Hound. You know him?" Mickey had no choice but to reveal a name now.

Lacy jarred his head and took a stern look at Mickey. *What the fuck these niggaz got going on*? Lacy thought.

He continued to look at Mickey in silence. His intention was to now know whether or not Hound had sent the guy his way. Lacy somewhat got pissed behind the notion. But then, he'd come to the conclusion that coincidences did happen, and that maybe this could be one of these particular scenarios playing itself out.

Ain't but one way to know exactly what is up, Lacy thought.

"Did Hound have the nerve to send you my way or something?" Lacy simply had to ask.

Mickey now jarred his head at Lacy following the question. He was confused.

"So, you two know one another, I assume?" Mickey asked.

"Yeah, we do. Me and Hound tight. He ain't never mention that to you?"

"Nah, he didn't. Had that been so, it would be him here tryna work a deal, and not me and Streetlife."

Mickey's clarity of words made sense to Lacy. He had no choice but to reason with them and continue to be logical.

"You got a good point. But fuck it! You say you got a hundred grand to spend, right? I can't let that type of money walk. How soon you looking to do this?" Lacy wanted to know.

"I'm a vampire, my nigga! I got the kind of energy to pull all-nighters if necessary. We can make this shit happen in the next hour if you want to. All I gotta do is run back to my pad, get the money, then make my way back here to see you. Is that what we doing?"

"Oh yeah. That's exactly what we doing. The sooner, the better. So, run on and do what you need to do. And by the time you've made it back, my people would have done all I need them to do and be back here for our deal to go down," stated Lacy.

"That's a bet! I'll be back shortly. And Streetlife can hold tight here with you until I do so. That's cool with you, Street?" asked Mickey.

"I ain't got no problem with none of that. Do what you do, player. Just make sure you do what you do by me as well, once everything is everything," Streetlife responded. "I'm here."

Mickey left out, got into his car, and drove about ten blocks to another location not far away and parked near a church. He then hopped out, opened the trunk and went into a secret compartment where he had money stashed away. He retrieved ten stacks, apparently ten thousand-dollar bundles each, and took a seat back in the car again. He brainstormed for a moment and pulled off, heading back near Lacy's bar.

Once there again, he parked down the street, at a distance on the opposite side. The intention was to sit and observe the people who moved in and out, personally contemplating whether he should return inside with that type of paper, or do without until Hound was to come through?

Mickey was the impatient type and demanded action when and how he saw fit, whether his decision making in those moments benefited him a little or cost him a lot by going the wrong way. He never moved when someone else thought he should. Especially not when it came to him being served.

Mickey allowed nearly an hour to pass with him looking on and thinking. Finally, he stepped out the car—money in tow—and headed to the entrance of the bar. He was yet again confronted by Lacy's security men, checked for weapons, and allowed to re-enter and escorted to the back-room office. Lacy and Streetlife awaited, sipping on bottles of suds. They had Old Milwaukee's Best.

"That didn't take too long," Lacy let out.

"It don't take long when you looking to do business. Especially for good product. Two things I'm serious about," responded Mickey.

"I know that's right," Lacy remarked. "And that's a hundred large you got in the bag there, right?"

"Ain't that's how much I say I was going to get? Now, what you got for me?"

Lacy took a pause with speaking. He looked at Mickey in an impressed way. No doubt, he already had knowledge that Mickey bought his supply from the Italian Don Angelo Marconi, the brother of the motherfucker who they'd jacked, and didn't know what the situation was between Mickey and Angelo to prevent him from going back for more supply. But there was one thing he knew for damn sure. It wasn't no goddamn guinea, who gave a nigga a hundred thousand dollars to come to him and buy product with from him. So, he knew it wasn't a set-up. That the money had to belong to Mickey. And that was for damn sure.

"It's a drought throughout the city. I'm sure you knowing this already. So, with that being the reality of the situation, I can't sell you nothing but three kilos. And I may put a four-way with it. But three units all you can get from me. Take it for the hundred Gee's or leave it. Your choice?" Lacy stated.

Mickey didn't even have to think long about it.

"I'll take it! Anything better than nothing right about now," he responded.

"You're a smart man, Mickey. I can't do nothing but respect that. But the truth is, once we do this deal here, you may have a bone to pick with your people, Hound. Or an ax to grind, even. He's holding back on you," Lacy insinuated.

"What! Why you say that?"

"He ain't keeping things on the up-and-up with you. I'mma tell you more in a minute." Lacy then produced the product.

Mickey stepped closer to the table where Lacy stood and the product sat. Lacy stabbed a knife into one of the kilos. A strong distinct odor permeated. Just as Mickey expected.

Lacy dug out a nice amount with the tip of the knife and passed off to Streetlife. He was the one designated to test the potency of the material. He snorted the heap through his nostrils.

"Oh yeah, Mickey. Good shit there! Real good shit, bro!" Streetlife confirmed, then began to nod from the effect of the drug.

Mickey passed Lacy the money and immediately began putting away the product he'd just bought.

"Now what was that you mentioned about Hound?" Mickey asked.

"I was definitely making it my business to tell you. The thing is this, Mickey. How he's your people and I assume business partner, and the nigga don't mention nothing to you at all about the goddamn dope he's sittin' on! That's all I wanna know," stated Lacy.

"What you mean by all that?"

"Maaan! That nigga got about thirty of them same kilos right there," he pointed at what he'd sold Mickey, "he holding onto. If you didn't know," Lacy informed.

"You got to be bullshittin' me!" Mickey was livid behind the thought of Hound holding back on him.

"Nah, Mickey, I'm shootin' straight with you, man. And when you see that nigga again, you be sure do tell that nigga I say he need to go on ahead and get off that shit! Because ain't no way those fucking pasta eating cutthroat guineas, got what it takes to retaliate against all of us now! That we win and they lose. And he better not come back my way again tryna tell me what the fuck to do with my portion of the take. That's what I need you to tell him," Lacy emphatically stated.

"I'll be sure to get him your message. But, about what me and you got going on, if need be, are you open for business again?" Mickey asked.

Lacy took a moment to think over the words his new customer asked of him. The answer he prepared was an easy one to give.

"As long as you spending this type of bread, hell yeah I am, nigga!" he let out, now thumbing through the rolls of money he held.

"Okay. Bet that up. And as promised, here you go, Streetlife. You gotta take the train or a cab back too. I'm going in the opposite direction," Mickey stated. He gave dude nearly an ounce of the product and fifty more dollars.

Mickey properly closed the bag that had the smack in it, shook Lacy's hand yet again, and made his way out of the bar to his vehicle. He was eager to get home and package up the narcotics for sale. His blood raced with anxiousness. His hands itched to get money hustling.

Chapter 8

Once home, Mickey immediately got on the phone and called Johnny Mack and Hound for an emergency meeting, saying that he needed to see them both ASAP! He now had product.

Nearly an hour later, the two cousins were there at Mickey's place. Throughout the time he awaited their arrival, he tinkered with the product to be sure the quality was as good as Streetlife proclaimed it to be. Heat was put to it, a small amount, and a light cut to stretch the dope. The H held up under each and every test. Lacy hadn't fucked him.

This some pretty good shit here, Mickey thought. "And it looks like I done had my hands on something like this before. Maybe so. I'll know sooner or later. But let me see now while I got the chance to."

Mickey lifted a wood panel from the flooring of the bathroom. He retrieved a kilo from the last two he had prior to connecting with Lacy. They'd come from Angelo. He made his way back to the kitchen table to make the comparison. The two separate batches of dope had the exact look, the exact texture, exact color, and the exact all else. Even the odor to it was the same.

Something fishy about this whole scenario. What the fuck really going on! he thought as the brainstorming intensified. *Now Hound seems to not want me to get in touch with Lacy. Lacy leaves a message he wants me to pass to Hound. A serious one at that! The shit I get from Lacy, looks like the same shit I got from Angelo. Angelo turned me away with my money and he ain't never done that. Then, he makes the claim he's busy tryna figure something out. Lacy makes mention about the guineas not being able to take on all of us at this point, that we win, they lose, and Hound sitting on thirty fuckin' kilos of H, and ain't said shit to me or Johnny Mack about it! I'm gonna get down to the bottom of this shit, tonight! Lord knows I am!*

Mickey thought over everything while the other two made their way to him.

Johnny Mack and Hound were let inside. The three went to the kitchen. The two took notice of the kilos Mickey had situated on the table.

"So, we back in business again. Who? Angelo?" asked Johnny Mack.

"Nah. Not him, Mack. I had to go to somebody else. A cat named 'Black Mafia Lacy' over in west Philly. Maybe Hound can school us on who he is and what he all about, since he's more familiar with him than we are, and since Lacy had a strong message that he wanted me to relate to him," Mickey responded. He and Johnny Mack rotated their heads and looked at Hound at the same time.

Hound jarred his head when Lacy's name was brought up.

"Mickey, yo impatient ass just couldn't wait until the weekend, could you?! But what was the message that that nigga had for me?" Hound wanted to know.

Mickey didn't hesitate to repeat Lacy's words. He was eager to hear what his cousin had to say. This would put him one step closer to knowing the truth of the matter.

"The nigga told me to tell you, that there wasn't no way that those fuckin' guineas had what it takes to go up against all of *us* now, that y'all win and they lose, and the last part to that was… you the one holding onto thirty or more kilos of the same shit he sold me! Now, what the fuck really going on, Hound? Me and Johnny Mack need to know. Because the shit I got from dude, gotta be some of the same shit I got from Angelo on the last trip to see him. And now, he claiming it ain't no more. So, shoot it straight to us, kinfolk! Tell us what the fuck going on! That way, we'll know what to expect and how to move going forward."

Mickey made a strong plea to Hound for him to ass-up on the information that needed to be known by him and Johnny Mack, for safety purposes, at least. They knew that the entire ordeal had something to do with the Italian Mafia of Philly, but not what exact group. Hound was being forced to fill in the blanks on that.

Mickey spoke out again before Hound was able to respond. There was something of serious nature he wanted to remind him of.

"And must me and Johnny Mack remind you, nigga! When your black ass was away, off in that goddamn chain-gang busting rocks, digging ditches, and building roads and shit, it was us of all people, who stood by your side the most and held you down like real cousins were supposed to. And when you got out, it was also us who put you on and provided you a solid way to do shit you like to do before you made a move and began to do your own thing. So—"

"—Basically nigga, we deserve to know the truth, Cornelius. And directly from you," Johnny Mack cut in to say.

Hound looked sternly at them both, one to the other. He knew they weren't going to let him off the hook so easily without him informing them about what was going on. And the only way he would be keeping it real with them as they had towards him, he needed to tell what was up, what had gone down. Mickey made it all make sense. Hound had to speak the truth. No matter what.

"Y'all want the truth?" Hound asked.

"Yeah, nigga!" Mickey and Johnny Mack let out together. They returned serious looks at him in doing so.

"A'ight, y'all got it. Here is what happened." Suspense built. He spoke. "Me and my Black Mafia niggaz made it our business to jack the mob for they shit!" Hound revealed.

"What the fuck!" Again, Mickey and Johnny Mack exclaimed at the same time.

Mickey spoke his mind first. "Nigga! Are you crazy?! What the fuck wrong with you, Hound?!?!"

"Shid nigga, for eighty keys of H, ninety grand, and four sweet pistols," he withdrew a .45 he had on him, "hell fuck yeah, I am! But, that clown-ass nigga, Lacy, done did too much talking, when he wasn't supposed to! He's put my life in danger now by running that mouth and going against what we agreed to do! And not only that. The nigga threatened me! So, we got a beef now. A score to settle. It ain't no forgetting about this and putting it away. He's gotta get it!" Hound spat.

"Hound! Me and Mickey need to know two things. What particular mob group y'all robbed? And, what all did y'all take?" the oldest of the three asked.

"We got the drop on a home that was being used as a stash spot. It belonged to Angelo's brother, Peter. So, you was right, Mickey. The dope did come from the Marconi guineas. And I just told you what all we got, Johnny Mack. It was eighty blocks of H, ninety grand, and four guns," Hound reiterated.

"Nigga! Y'all stuck-up Angelo's brother and took his dope from him! That's Angelo's shit, Hound!" Mickey said vehemently.

"It *was* Angelo's shit! But not anymore. And that old fuck Peter, wasn't home when we hit. The wife was. We made that bitch tell us where everything was hidden. She was caught down bad back in the backyard. No need to worry though. We were covered good from head to toe. They don't have a clue on who it possibly was to get 'em. Don't know where to begin looking," Hound explained.

"Okay, Hound. What's done is done. We can't continue to back track about it. But do you realize how serious this shit is you now involved in? This some pretty deep shit, fam. Real talk," Mickey said.

"Mickey, again, they don't have a clue on who did what, or how we got information on what they had in the house and where it was located. I just don't appreciate the fact of how that nigga Lacy, made it his business to put our business out there like that. But I don't wanna keep talking about it. Y'all tryna do business or what?" Hound stated. He appeared to declare a new position with his demeanor and all he said.

"You already know we tryna do some business. That was already understood before we found out all we now know. But, we need to understand where you stand with us from this point moving forward. Because clearly, there's a lot of things that have changed. Clearly there is," said Mickey.

"What you mean by that, *where I stand with y'all?* What's that, a trick question or something? I answered the call you made that you wanted to meet. I'm here, ain't I? I'm family. But I'm also in position to do my own thing now. I'm gonna build my own team. And I'm hoping we can keep our teams tied together for the long haul. How y'all feel about that?" Hound responded.

"Hound, if I may, let me make some sense for you about a thing or two. The shit you took from Angelo and 'em, it's only gonna last so long. How you plan to re-up when you run out? That's what I wanna know," Mickey let out.

"Shit! I already know that I ain't got no choice but to try and find a connect to keep me supplied. I'll have plenty of bread to do so with. And at the same time, your door to Angelo, Mickey, will more than likely be open once more. Then I can put my money with y'all money like we always do, and keep the ball rolling like that," Hound responded. He was very logical with the way he explained the next move he was to make.

"And you think it's just that easy, huh?" Johnny Mack chimed in to ask.

"If it's one thing I done came to learn, kinfolk, money makes everything easy! I know this for a fact! And I'mma be out there on them corners," he pointed towards the outside world at large, "getting money and doing all we do. Because me, y'all, and the group of niggaz I got lined up with me, don't know nothing else but to make bread, and make other outside niggaz get down or lay it down behind our cause. And if I ain't doing proper business with my family, that could send the wrong message to niggaz on the outside looking in. Y'all feel where I'm coming from on that?" Hound explicitly put it.

Johnny Mack felt the need to speak to the words Hound spoke.

"Hound, ain't no doubt about it, we're all good on our end. The Savage family that is. And I don't see why you can't do your own thing and build your own team outside of what we got going on as family. I'm pretty sure there won't be a situation where the two sides will bump heads leaving you caught up in the middle. But enough on those lines. Where that dope at you got stashed, nigga?! Me and Mickey got money to spend. What we get for three hundred thousand?" he asked emphatically.

"Three hundred thousand, huh, Mickey?" he called out and looked him dead in the eyes. "What that nigga Lacy sell you each kilo for?"

"He sold me three and maybe four ounces more for a hundred large," Mickey replied.

"Okay. So, for the both of you together, I'll give y'all twelve bricks. The three extras are my repayment to y'all niggaz, for everything y'all gave me and did for me when I was down bad in prison. Now, y'all won't be able to throw that shit up in my face no more, as I'll be done re-paid y'all back, and far more than y'all gave me," Hound stated.

"That's a bet," said Mickey.

"Now take your ass on and get that goddamn work you holding onto. And me and Mickey gonna be right here with the money when you get back! And no matter what you do, Cornelius, or how high you rise in your quest for power and glory, don't let it change you in a negative way. Be sure to keep family first, know who you are as a man and the man the family made you. Never let nothing or no one take you away from that. A'ight?" Johnny Mack stated. He always spoke real and raw to his younger cousins.

The three slapped fives and hugged one another. Hound then made his way out the door to go and get the kilos of H he was set to sell to his people.

***

Meanwhile...
As Hound was away, Mickey and Johnny Mack continued to talk. No doubt, Hound was the topic of the discussion.

"Mickey. I sure as hell hope we ain't got a problem on our hands with Hound now. He got a lot of shit going on. But I'm still curious to know, how the fuck did that nigga get the inside scoop to know where the dope was situated, and on where Angelo's brother live?" Johnny Mack stated.

"Beats the shit outta me. But truth is, them niggaz hit good! My only concern is, what's to happen once those goddamn Italians get word who's the people that got all the H in circulation around town?" Mickey responded.

"A damn race-war could pop off! All over some illegal shit at that! Them mob muthafucka's' gonna go to whacking niggaz left and right. Niggaz that ain't got shit to do with nothing. You watch and see. Mark my words."

The conversation went on and got deeper as they awaited Hound. No one knew what to expect in the near future, or what was to come. The element of surprise of what the future had in store, was enough to scare anybody who had a beef with the mob. Mickey's only hope was that his name wouldn't get caught up in the rapture of what was to occur.

Chapter 9

Over In Little Italy...

Angelo and his men managed to gather enough of the right information necessary, to narrow the search on "who pulled the caper" on them and took what they had. He also had Marconi foot soldiers out and about in known areas throughout the city where heroin was rampant. Whether that be in Italian neighborhoods, in the whites, Latino, or black ghetto havens, they were determined to know who had more narcotics in circulation than the other. Then, what do you know? It was made known that the black dope holes out in west Philly won the contest.

Angelo's guys were then sent out to west Philly to shop with the dealers who had baggies on retail. They also had orders to spend time inside the dope house to learn more about the main man who supplied the spots. The mobsters posing as junkies, actually turned and blessed the real addicts with the drugs, money, and other material things in exchange to talk more. Time after time, the same names continued to pop up. The "Black Mafia Boys," and some big mouth cat named "Lacy" who loved to brag and talk cold shit.

Angelo had a very loyal and dedicated capo named Joey, the one from before when they'd first did business with Mickey and crew. He made it his business to send out three of his best soldiers to three different drug houses, on three different days, being that he now had knowledge they belonged to Black Mafia or either Lacy. They each bought an ounce of H. When the material was brought back to him, he immediately knew that it was from the batch that they'd last had. There were a few kilos left in his possession, and the comparisons were made. Indeed, he had a match. He ran to Angelo with the discovery.

"So, you mean to tell me that the product these monkeys are selling belongs to us?" stated Don Angelo.

"That's exactly what it all boils down to, Don," Joey responded.

"I now need to find out who provided the information to where my brother lives? And not only that. How did they know what was inside? I only hope that we don't have a leak somewhere inside this family's structure."

"We shall continue to get to the bottom of this, Don. We definitely will."

"You better! Because I don't wish to speculate on a thing. And heads are gonna soon roll, yo hear me! You're my top capo, Joey. Security is a main priority. We have a problem now. Peter's house could've easily been my house. And Sylvia could've easily been my wife who was there that day. I'm entrusting you to be the one to find and eliminate this threat we now experience with this family. Our safety has been breached. Don't let this fall on you. It's a must you make this right, in as fast a manner as you possibly could! You have my permission to terminate anyone you deem that had anything to do with this, or anyone who knew about the plot and didn't report them to us. Just be sure to have the evidence to support your actions on whom you point the finger at. And don't be sloppy in your duty. As you're aware, my brother Peter is the underboss of this family. His wife's sister is dead. And their beloved doggie is too. Sylvia is terrified out of her mind. The actions of these people spell war. We've got a skunk in our camp. Someone who passed off information to have the job done. That's treason. And we can't have that. Understood!" Don Angelo gave a lengthy monologue. He basically vented to Joey.

"I know and understand your concerns, Don, and I shall get the results you expect of me in due time. I already have an idea on where else to look, and who to single out. I can't have this terrible situation fall on me."

"And who or where might that be? Whom are you singling out, and where you looking first?" asked Don Angelo.

"Please allow me the opportunity to be sure before I am to mention a name, Don," Joey replied. He stood to his feet and readied himself to leave the presence of Don Angelo. "Nonetheless, Don, my wrath shall begin immediately, with those wretched niggers, who I know has our product in their possession," Joey lastly declared and exited the room. He went to do work.

***

Two Weeks Later...

Capo Joey made it his business to utilize one of his Italian female workers who danced topless at one of the taverns he managed that was owned by the Marconi family. Her name was Victoria. She was the perfect example of what Italian beauty was supposed to look like. She had long flowing dark hair, dark brown eyes, evenly tan olive complexioned skin, and a slim tight figure. Victoria was five-six in height and kept her weight between a hundred ten and a hundred twenty pounds. Her lovely set of boobs and curvy butt matched. Neither were too large nor too undeveloped. Her looks and figure determined her income and type of livelihood she lived. There was a duty to keep herself proper.

Joey ordered Victoria to forge an acquaintance with a Negro hood out of west Philly. He had a supply of heroin they were getting rich from. He and his cronies. She was to develop an affair with the guy. His name was Lacy, she'd been told. Trust needed to be established. That way, her brother "Joey," might be able to spend his money with a supplier as the drought continued to drag on, and business would go as usual. Joey wanted to buy two kilos of heroin but had no one to deal them to him.

This was the plot put together so to snag Lacy at the opportune moment.

Joey had a Negro associate of his he ran the numbers games with. It was he who provided Joey with critical inside information on where the exact hangout was Lacy favored to socialize. Turns out, with Lacy being "new money" and thought of himself having a bit of class and sophistication, he'd developed a taste for the finer things life had to offer. Therefore, his social habits changed, and he'd moved from the party havens in the ghetto he was all too familiar with, to the downtown locations where a diverse crowd of affluent ladies and gentlemen toast wine, puff expensive cigars, take care of their exclusive drug appetites in private, and even cut business deals, both legitimate and illegitimate ones. This made the situation smoother for Joey to send Victoria the gorgeous, his way. Nothing would appear out the ordinary.

There existed a social lounge called "Gio's" at the time. It was located in downtown Philly, Center City. The site offered people of all races and ethnicities the opportunity to have fun and express themselves the way they liked. With the passing of the Civil Rights Bill of 1964, blacks could now celebrate and be joyous alongside whites and let the good times roll. Interracial relations and fellowship were at an all-time high.

And so, with a pretty and sexy Italian female in a lovely form-fitting dress approaching a black man in Gio's because he became of interest to her, was not looked down upon nor caused a ruckus as would have during the times of the past. This was how Victoria was able to get an angle and make a move on Lacy.

Over the week-long time period from the night in Gio's when they met, the two had been out on a date twice. Victoria also was able to provide a blow job to hook him further and made it possible for Lacy to lower his defense. He held no more suspicion of her as he would have had she continued to hold back intimately.

The two hooked up yet again on this particular Saturday night. For all it was worth, Victoria signaled to him through seductive and arousing body language, that they would indeed be having sex, once they returned to the hotel suite Lacy reserved.

Once there in the privacy of the lodge Lacy paid top dollar to parlay in for the weekend, basically looking to impress Victoria. They were between rounds of sex and lay on the bed and began to pillow talk over a few things.

For some reason unknown to man, at any time a black guy finds himself in an intimate situation with a non-black female, he always tends to become more 'laxed in his ways and loose at the lips. So much so to the point that he'd blabber endlessly about all his business and all he had plans to do. Black guys are forever seeking to impress and fascinate females, rather than have the female do so unto him. This was exactly what Lacy did, and had no clue that Victoria was working for the ops.

The two lay asshole naked atop the bed. The vocals of a sensational female jazz singer emitted from the radio. Victoria wanted to talk. She lowered the volume to where music still could be heard, but barely.

"I see you're doing well for yourself these days, Lacy. Moving a lot of product, I assume? That's a good thing. An attractive Italian sweetheart as myself, does deserve special treatment that a man has to offer. And I am, a special kind of girl, you know," she purred in his ear sensuously, then nibbled on the lobe with her lipstick coated lips.

"Oh yeah. You the type of female I can really grow with and come to appreciate. Your beauty and your sex appeal motivates me in a major way. Also, I'm doing my thing out there in those streets. I might be the only muthafucka' in all of Philly, who got plenty of H to sell. And I'm having that shit my way! I got kilos of it!" Lacy began to boast on his underworld business without any sense of being cautious at the mouth.

"Oh, you're having it your way you say, huh? I like the sound of that. I wouldn't want a man to be no less than one of the top men, while he's in my life. That's why I chose you from the flock, Lacy." Victoria wooed him with her choice of words and charm.

Lacy smiled like he'd never done before at the compliments.

Victoria continued. "I would like to know more about your business and the product you sell. I'm sure I will be able to add to you or even help create a way that we can offer your material to those in my community who have a desire for it. Italians like to get high too, ya know" she said.

Lacy looked at her. A bulb lit up in his head due to an idea he now had. He knew eventually he'd run out of the material he had and would need to connect with a supplier to keep things going. The Italians had strong ties to the suppliers of the French Connection. And now that he had an Italian female in his life, he reasoned, the possibility existed that she could be utilized to plug him with the heavy Italian dealers who were getting it into the country. And there wasn't a doubt in his mind that it would be these same suppliers, to once again flood the streets of Philly with dope in due time.

He knew many names of people. He knew many places that sold heroin. And he knew about many things that the underworld Italian mafioso had going on. This was learned by being with Hound during the times before they pulled the caper. Lacy was looking to capitalize on the information and to continue to rise to power.

"Victoria. I'm curious to know something. You familiar with any of those mob dudes who roam in south Philly? Or of Angelo Marconi's people?"

She gave him a hard look following the question.

"And why would you automatically assume I may know someone who's in the mob?"

"Because, babe, you a different type. Not from ordinary stock either. Also, you said it. You may be able to add to me and help create a way that we could offer my product in your community for those who got a desire for it. This is the way I want you to help me create a way. By connecting me to someone who has connections to a supply line of heroin. I'm gonna eventually need more smack, baby girl. And soon. And you gonna be the one to make this happen for me." Lacy made a demand then and there.

"I may know a person or two. But you should already know that mafioso men are really skeptical about doing business with black guys. Especially business of that nature," Victoria responded.

"And that's the area where you come in at."

"Well, if that be so, I'm definitely going to need more information about a few things. I'm sure the people I know, are going to want to know more about the person I'm looking to connect with them."

"Information like what?" asked Lacy.

"You said you've got kilos, right? So obviously, you already have a supplier."

"Nope! Never had a supplier at no time," Lacy stated emphatically. "But look, here's the deal. I'm 'Black Mafia,' Victoria. We a new wave of gangsta's that's taking over Philly. And the bottom line is that we take what we want! This how we make our living to get where we need to be. Status-wise that is. The way I came up on those kilos I got, me and my crew jacked a warehouse for them. The place was owned by some Italian cats. It was another Italian dude who provided the info so we could get the drop on the location. It was some guy I ain't seen since. He might be dead for all I know," Lacy revealed. "I only seen him once. He and my former partner had a conversation."

"And what was his name?" she made a gamble by asking.

"A guy named Neil. 'Nimble Neil,' was what they called him. Now how he got that name? I have no idea."

"So, I can only assume that the guy Neil, had to rely upon non-Italian men, to do the deed? So, to keep the heat from him?"

"That about sums it up. Preserve life at all costs is the number one rule of survival. The guy had to keep his name clear, to keep from getting whacked! Eighty fuckin' kilos of H, ninety K in cash, and a few weapons, probably would have had him pulled apart in 'five' different ways, and then, his body parts dumped in the river! He was a smart man to do it that way. And that was a smart move," Lacy said.

"And Neil is a member of which family?"

"At the time, he was only an associate of Scalia. I'm sure they have made him by now. The caper we pulled for the material belonged to Marconi. An old geezer named Peter. The Scalia's were done a favor by us. We helped them by putting a strain on the Marconi's money. That was a whole 'lotta shit we took! Made me a rich man, Victoria," Lacy confessed.

"That's a well-known fact in Italian Philly. That the Scalia's and Marconi's are bitter rivals."

"And that made the job much easier for us, to do what we needed to do, leaving Marconi pointing the finger at their enemy. We capitalized off the beef they have. You know what I mean."

"I do," Victoria answered, then got to her feet from the bed and began to get dressed. "I'm hungry, Lacy. I've got a taste for Italian food. I know a diner on my side of town that serves twenty-four seven. I'm gonna go and get us something to eat. I'm taking your car. I'll be back shortly, okay?" she said and grabbed her purse, his car keys, then exited the suite.

Victoria made her way directly to where Joey was located. She had a lot of information on hand to provide.

Chapter 10

One Hour Later...

Victoria met Joey at the diner she'd mentioned going to. He escorted her to the backspace of the eatery. They took a seat at the table and got down to business. She dug into her purse to pull out the mini tape recorder that was there. The entire time she and Lacy lay and talked, it was being captured by the device.

"What you got for me on this baboon!" Joey asks and grimaces at the thought.

"Everything you want to know. Have a listen for yourself," she responded, then pressed play to roll the tape.

Joey heard all there was. And to his advantage, he also knew who the guy Nimble Neil was too. Joey made the connections to it all. At least as much as he could.

"Where is this monkey at now?"

"He's still at the hotel. Room three ten," she revealed. "And I have his car. It's out front."

"You keep put. Give me the keys to his car. I've got something in store for that jungle-bunny!" Joey spat.

He departed the diner, got into his car, had one of his soldiers drive Lacy's, and they headed to another location to prepare and make a move on Lacy while they had him with his pants off and down bad. Joey was intent on getting the help of his most trusted goombahs.

***

Thirty Minutes Later ...
Joey, and two other powerful men of Philly, were now at the door of the hotel suite where Lacy lay. They banged on the door prior to barging in on forced entry.
"Philadelphia Police! Freeze asshole!" one of the officers yelled out. He had his gun drawn and trained on Lacy.
"You're under arrest!"
Lacy jumped up from the bed and threw his hands up high. He was still in the nude.
"What the fuck! Under arrest! For what?" Lacy retorted.
"Shut the fuck up, boy! We do all the questioning here!" the second cop exclaimed, roughly grabbing Lacy by the arms and slapping cuffs on his wrists. His manhood swayed left to right from his brief moment of resisting.
"What am I being arrested for?" Lacy asked again. He got no response.
Moments later, in walked Joey. He didn't say a word. He tosses Lacy his drawers and pants. They were each put on. The three men then escort Lacy from the room, through the lobby, and out the door to an unmarked car. Lacy was under the impression that a squad car was awaiting to put him in to be taken to the station. However, there wasn't one. He was harshly shoved into the back seat with Joey sitting beside him.
"Yo, what the fuck going on!" Lacy barked.
Wham!
Joey socked him in the mouth with a right hook.
"Shut the fuck up, nigger! That's what you do!" spat Joey.
The off-duty cop Joey had on his payroll that was doing the driving, steered the vehicle to a remote location just on the outskirts of the city near the Delaware River. They got out and dragged Lacy from the back seat in the process. They dragged him by the legs down to the muddy bank and situated him on his knees.

"So, muthafucka'! You wanna have the balls to jack me and my people for our product, huh?" Joey said.

Wham!

He punched him hard, in the nose this time. "If you plan on living to see tomorrow, nigger, you best get to talking! Who else was involved? Who helped you with the robbery job done on the home of Peter Marconi?"

Joey now had Lacy in a chokehold from behind and yanked him from side-to-side like a rag doll.

"Talk, nigger! Talk I say!" Joey further barked.

Wham!

One of the other police henchmen viciously slammed a tire rod into Lacy's chest. At least four ribs were broken in the process. Lacy fell over to one side. He coughed up a thick glob of blood.

Joey yanked Lacy from the ground back to his knees. He then slapped him.

Whop!

"Spit it out, nigger! What you know!"

Whop!

"Talk! Who done it with you!"

"I don't know what you talkin' 'bout. Turn me loose!" Lacy responded best he could.

"You fucking nigger! Victoria recorded everything you said to her in the hotel room! How you think I know where to find you? So, stop lying to me, you fucking monkey!"

Joey then played some of the recording.

Whop!

"Now give me names! And where's the rest of our product y'all took?" Joey demanded to know.

Joey then snatched a revolver from the hands of one of the others, pulled back on the hammer, and pressed the tip of the barrel under Lacy's left eye.

Lacy spoke out. "So, you had that sleazy slut Victoria, set me up, huh? I shoulda' known she was too good to be true. But what I gotta say is this. It wasn't my idea. I wasn't the leader. Nimble Neil and Hound Savage were. Those two shoulda' been your targets. Not me," Lacy admitted. But why?

Joey looked on at the two men he had with him. His head and eyes went from left-to-right rapidly. He searched for confirmation on the names.

"Neil is Scalia now, I'm aware," one of them worded.

"I'm familiar with Neil. But, who's the other?" Joey responded. He then had a brief thought to himself. *Where do I recall the name Savage?*

"Hound Savage! Which family? Ain't but three in Philly."

"He's ain't Italian. He's black! And is my Black Mafia brother. Hound don't play the radio either. He's a straight killer! So, once you begin trying to hunt him down, he's gonna be doing the same to you."

Finally, the Savage name dawned upon him.

"Any ties between the Hound guy and Mickey Savage?" Joey asked.

"They related and got strength and pull in the streets like no other! So, when you kill me, you might as well go on ahead and begin counting down your last days as well, you fuckin' oily hair having fake Mafia muthafucka'! Now go suck on a sick dog's dick, you guinea fuck-boys!" Lacy defiantly spat.

"Oh yeah! How about yo suck on this dog's dick! This forty-four Bulldog I got here!" Joey countered.

He rammed the pistol into Lacy's mouth and pulled the trigger.

Boom!

The force from the blast jarred Lacy's head violently. His body slowly fell backwards down to the mud.

Boom! Boom! Boom!

Joey shot him three more times for good measure, one in the face and twice in the chest. The thick slug knocked a chunk of bone and flesh from Lacy's forehead. He was killed without a drop of mercy shown. Lacy's days were no more.

His reign in the streets was short lived. Had he only kept that fucking big mouth of his closed from spewing his business, and not become so desperate for a piece of Italian pussy, he'd still be alive to see the remainder of those kilos he had get done. Also, he would have had the opportunity to see his son grow and come of age. But, his end arrived, leaving a portion of the assailants eliminated that had jacked Angelo. The mob prevailed.

Chapter 11

Several Weeks Later...

Miss Peaches gave birth to a son while locked away in the Dade County Jail. She made it her absolute business to name the baby directly after the father, Robert Francis Kavanaugh II. He was Bobby's first and only son. The little one carried many features of the father, but for the most part, the darker complexion of skin was taken from the mother.

Mickey had Sparkle travel down south to Miami to get the baby and deliver him to the custody of Peaches's mother in Savannah on her way back to the north. The mother would be the one to care after him until Peaches eventually came from under the legal ordeal she battled and be able to have her child to herself from that point.

Once Mickey was contacted by Peaches and made aware of her baby being brought into the world, he was sure to hire a lawyer to represent her and help speed up the process to get her free. Her detainment was illegal. The charges trumped up against her were bogus to begin with. Bobby coerced the D.A. there in Miami to hold her basically, as Mickey wasn't a wanted fugitive for the charge of "Aiding and Abetting" against Peaches to stick.

The charges were eventually dropped behind the work of the attorney, and she was freed. Through it all, the hardest part for Peaches was to have her baby while in a jail cell, from a man who was now an enemy, and tried to kill them both. Her loyalty and commitment had and was always to

Mickey first over anybody else. And those qualities couldn't have been put to the test more than at that time. He owed her big. And the type of payment Peaches had in mind was one he could possibly agree with. She was back in Philly and the two talked.

"I want that fuckin' dirty low-down, trash-ass white boy dead, Mickey! You hear me! Dead as a fuckin' doorknob! And I mean that shit!" Peaches vent. "That nasty cracka' gotta die! For the old and the new! Now either we gonna get him together, or I'll do so without you. What's it gonna be, Mickey?!"

She laid an ultimatum. One that wasn't to be denied.

"Peaches! I want that piece of shit dead myself. Probably more than you do. But here's the thing. We gotta figure out a way to get the drop on him without it getting out who it was. He ain't no sitting lame-duck, you know. Bobby has much power now. And can easily have us killed one of many ways, but in particular, by the police, or by way of the death penalty if we were to get caught for killing him. So, we gotta think this through," Mickey responded in his signature diplomatic style.

"Mickey, you always on this 'use your head and think first type shit,' dude! That's jive to me! That bastard tried to kill you, me, and the baby! His own damn son! Thank God he didn't hit me in the belly with that bullet! But for him shooting me anyway, he's gotta go! Period!"

There seemed to be no end to Peaches's anger and venting.

"And go, he shall do. Once I think this thing through. However, you do know that you got the power now to do a lot more harm to Bobby than you know, right? That's if you really want to?" Mickey said.

"And how is that? Because I'm tired of talking and thinking things through when it comes to this bastard! The time for action is now, Mickey! And I mean it!" Peaches spat.

"We gonna do the same thing we been doing. Only in a different way."

"I'm still waiting for you to say how?" she retorted.

"Through blackmail, Peaches. We gonna blackmail that fucka like never before. That's how."

"Mickey, I'mma be all the way real with you here about this. Because I've always believed in you and have never doubted not for once. This next plan you so-call yourself, you got cooking, it better work. Like for real, it better, in order for me to keep my belief in you. Things are different at this point. That motherfucker tried to kill me and my baby! I know he was intending to shoot me in my belly. But do I need to keep reminding you of that until I can't no more? Our next move must be an effective one. We need to gain an edge of him. That's what we need to do."

Mickey looked sternly at her. He knew that she'd gotten older on him and wiser in her thinking. This made it harder for him to maintain that certain level of control over her as he had in all those years. But at the same time, Peaches had more value to him now than at any other period throughout their acquaintance. Therefore, he definitely needed to take heed of all she'd said, so as to cash in on the particular ploy he had in mind.

Mickey spoke in a cozy manner to make her feel better. "Miss Peaches, truthfully, I have no choice but to show you now better than I can tell you. How does that sound? And, you know I've always delivered on my word. I've never let you down. This time ain't no different. All I need for you and Sparkle to do is..." She was also there. He pointed back and forth between them both. "...continue to listen to me and continue to let me lead the way. Just like we always operated. I don't need any backtalk. I don't need any disrespect. And I don't need y'all not doing what I tell y'all to do. All I need y'all to do is continue to mind me to the highest level you can. Do I make that clear?" Mickey let out with a tinge of anger to his voice.

Miss Peaches poked out her lips and appeared somewhat reluctant to answer up. But nonetheless, she did.

"Yes Mickey. You make that clear."

Sparkle then complied. "Yes, daddy. I understand. You make that clear."

"Good! Now you two listen up …" Mickey went on explaining what the next move was to be against Bobby Kavanaugh. He didn't hold by his wrath in words.

***

Meanwhile...

Joey reported back to Don Angelo with the news of him having terminated at least one of the perpetrators who stole their product. He presented the recording from Victoria as well. Joey wanted the Don to hear for himself.

"This is outstanding work, Joey. However, we now need to know who the 'Neil' guy and the 'Hound Savage' idiot is. Any idea where we may be able to gain a scent on their trail? No pun intended either. And are they both of Italian blood?" the Don wanted to know.

"I'm afraid they're not, Don Angelo. Only one. The other is a spade. What I've learned is that there were three spades who robbed the underboss' house. So, we got one down with three more to go. That's the other two nigger monkeys and the Italian traitor who provided the information," Joey responded.

"You know what I want? I want you and all the other capos to locate the Italian first … 'Nimble Neil' … as he seems to be the source to it all. And when y'all do eventually get him, for him to tell you all you need to know. I want you to snip a finger at a time or a toe, until he 'fesses up, or one after another. And once he does what you need him to do, at that point, you whack away his head and bring it to me … on a platter! That way, I may find some sort of satisfaction for all he's done in attack against this family. I took their actions personally, Joey. I'm hurt behind this," Don Angelo stated.

"There may be a slight issue down the line with this, Don Angelo."

"How so?"

"This guy Nimble Neil was only a Scalia associate at the time. I'm sure he's been made by now."

"If this be so, that can only mean the Scalia family authorized a move against us. And that violates the peace treaty that was in place, and we agreed upon. But, I don't care! That scumbag took from our family, someone died in the process behind this. How are we to get even? How is Scalia to justify these actions? They can't. So, whatever the outcome is to be, it is to be. Now you get me this Nimble Neil guy! And I want him taken care of soon. Along with the other two niggers who play a part. And in the meantime, I'll ask around about him myself. Now, please leave me," the Don concluded.

Chapter 12

Joey left the presence of his leader and set out on the mission to do more work. He ordered an immediate meeting between him and all the soldiers on his watch. That meant that Rocco and his brother Tony had to be there. They were the two who knew Hound the most, as Rocco was the one who brought Hound to them on business to begin with.

Joey opened up and began to brief his men on the new assignment that they were to do.

"Fellas, we have an urgent and important mission from Don Angelo. There's two pieces of shit that's marked for death, an Italian cut-throat named 'Nimble Neil' and a fucking 'Shine' by the name 'Hound Savage.' Any one of you heard of them?"

Rocco jarred his head at the mention of the names. Especially that of Hound, being that he was considered a friend and business acquaintance. But, the mafia family that he'd swore to give his life to protect, was dealt a blow that couldn't be overlooked or ignored. They'd been violated in a major way. And, Rocco ran the risk of losing his own life, had he not spoken out truthfully to the questions put to them by Joey. He simply had to speak up.

"I'm aware of them both," Rocco responded.

"Oh you are? Well maybe you could tell us more then, couldn't you?" Joey said.

"Absolutely I could …"

Rocco related all he knew.

Turns out, Neil had a female he dated on the regular. They had a deeply involved sexual affair going on. This particular female was employed with the municipal government of the city at Philadelphia Gas, Lights, and Water Department. Rocco had knowledge of this as well through a brief conversation he and Neil shared. Neil bragged to him about having a young hot piece of ass who works there. "At any time she was working him with a good blow job, or in reverse-cowgirl while she takes on the huge cock he has. He couldn't get enough of Tracy," Neil even mentioned a name, "and had to have her at every chance he could."

The idea was that, if they were to get to Tracy, kidnap her, and beat the girl good, that eventually, she'd tell all she knew about Neil, leaving no stone unturned in doing so. Rocco once saw a photo of Tracy and somewhat knew what she looked like.

Joey and Rocco arrived at Tracy's place of work at 4:00 p.m. She was due to end her day shortly. The two scoped out the surrounding area beforehand, to have a smooth getaway once the moment became the moment.

Theresa came walking out of the building. She was completely oblivious of all there was in store for her.

"That's Theresa right there, Joey," Rocco stated, pointing a finger at the same time.

She had on a floral pattern light blue dress with a waist tie strap to it.

"Is that right?" Joey squinted his eyes in a fit of anger at the sight of the female. He was behind the wheel of the car they'd utilized.

Joey kept his eyes trained on Theresa as she was heading towards her car, to know what her car looked like, so they could make their move before she'd gotten to it.

Theresa approached a dark gray sports car. A Dodge. She dug into her purse for the keys and was in the process of unlocking the door. Joey pulled up behind her, seemingly at the precise point her key touched the door lock. The back passenger door to Joey's car was already open with Rocco eager to snatch her.

Joey jammed on the brakes, causing the tires to screech. This startled Tracy. She turned to see what was going on. Rocco took action.

Wham!

He whacked her on the head with a foot-long metal wrench.

Down hard to the pavement she went behind the blow. She was out cold. Possibly near dead.

Rocco grabbed hold of her thin body, lifted her from the pavement, and aggressively tossed her onto the backseat of the car they rode in. Her purse was still strapped to her shoulder. Rocco tied her up to prevent a struggle and slapped her around because he could.

Joey drove to a location in south Philly where he intended to torture Tracy. It was a small home he owned that had a garage to it. The basement was damn near soundproof. A perfect situation to prevent her screams for help being heard.

The predator duo yanked their prey from the car and dragged her by the legs across the concrete floor of the garage from one point to the next. Her backside and head scraped harshly.

"Rocco, smack this cunt around a little to help her come to," Joey ordered. The blow to the head had really done a number on her.

It took Theresa nearly twenty minutes or so to come around. Phase two was to begin at that point. Rocco sat her up to an Indian-style position on the floor. Her back was against the wall to prevent her from falling backwards. She was still disoriented. No words were uttered by her. Joey began with his questions.

"In case you're wondering why we done this to you and why are you here, I wanna know who the fuck is 'Nimble Neil!' The boyfriend of yours? So, if you looking to live, I suggest you talk!"

Theresa had something important to say. Something her abductors hadn't prepared for.

"You've made a huge mistake. My father is a made man, I can tell you. And if you don't let me go, he's gonna have your heads. The both of you. I can promise that," she warned.

Joey and Rocco looked at her and laughed vehemently. It was now Joey's turn to be hands-on in his introduction.

Whop!

He smacked her hard about the face.

"Bitch! Who the fuck is Neil! Tell us that!" he spat.

Whop!

He smacked her again for good measure.

"Talk! And we might let you live. But if you don't, then you shall surely die!" he further stated. "It's that simple. Fuck whoever your father is! We couldn't care less!"

Whop!

"Okay-okay! I've had enough. Neil is an ex-boyfriend of mine. We no longer see each other, because he moved away. I haven't seen him in a while now. Months even. He's only called. That's about it," Theresa responded.

"Where did he go?" asked Joey.

Theresa panted in exhale, then answered. "He moved to Pittsburgh. He said he has family there. But he's a made man now himself and is to return to Philadelphia soon."

"And when was the last time you talked to this dickhead?"

"What was his reason for going to Pittsburgh?"

"To work, he said."

"What type of work? Don't lie to me either."

"I honestly have no idea. All I know is, it has to be some type of get rich quick scheme. He keeps a lot of cash on hand. Neil blessed me with five thousand dollars before he left," Theresa revealed.

"Does he deal drugs? Heroin maybe?" Joey now began to get very specific.

"Possibly. He said he also needed to leave to prevent a war from breaking out. That there was a battle brewing for product and territory."

"A break-out war between who? And what product and territory? Be specific!" demanded Joey.

"Neil is aware my father is of the Marconi family. He's tied to the Scalia group and —"

"Who is your father, bitch?" Joey immediately cut her off to ask.

"My father's name is Dolan … Dolan Estafan. He's the driver for Peter Marconi. And if you don't turn me loose right now, he and his people are gonna have your asses!" she vehemently spat. "He and his crew will hunt you down like there's no tomorrow!"

Both Joey and Rocco took stern looks at one another. They were petrified now from fear. They knew then and there that they'd fucked up. And in a major way. They couldn't walk back the drastic acts perpetrated against Tracy. She'd made them aware of too much through the line of questions they'd asked. Also, if they were to let her go, she would surely go to her father to report what all had happened to her. Theresa had seen their faces, and the car Joey drove as well. The death of the two was a guarantee if Theresa was freed, as their actions against her couldn't be justified no type of way. They'd done too much and now had to reap what they'd sown. Or …

Click-clack!

Boom! Boom-Boom-Boom!

Joey withdrew his nine-millimeter pistol, round one in the chamber, then shot Theresa in the head and chest area. He didn't care about the fact of her being the one and only of a made man. Whether the father being part of the same crime family as he, Joey didn't give a shit at that point. A decision had to be made, and his was to simply kill her. The father will never know.

Rocco, Joey's longtime friend and soldier, only stood and looked in utter silence. They were no closer to the truth of knowing who Neil was than they were prior to abducting and murdering Tracy.

"We now gotta find the time to head out to Pittsburgh to track down the Neil fucker, Rocco. Gotta clean up this mess here first," Joey declared.

"Yeah... I guess you're right. We don't have a choice now, do we?"

They now had to continue with having one another's back from that point. There was enough trust between them to know that the other wouldn't say a word, least the both of them would be killed, as opposed to only one. They'd done the deed together. Therefore, one hand had to wash the other, so they both could continue to live.

They each took hold of a hacksaw and began to dismember Tracy's body. They'd cut the poor girl into many different pieces. She died an ugly violent death, and no trace was left of her.

***

One Day Later...

Don Angelo attempted to contact Mickey. He had no success in doing so, although he'd personally made repeated efforts. He wanted to ask of "Mickey Savage," did he know of another black guy who went by the name "Hound Savage?" The surname of the two wasn't so common amongst the people. There simply had to be a relation, so thought the Don.

He became angry at Mickey not being the one answering his phone, especially when there was a need to. This now made him more suspicious of Mickey, and such questioning of him had not occurred at any time they'd done business with one another. And being that Mickey hadn't long before the day came to him with a large amount of cash, looking to buy more heroin. And now, he couldn't be contacted. Something wasn't right, and Don Angelo sought to know what it was.

That fucking black monkey! He must have bought the product he was looking for, from the other monkey, who shared the same family name as him, Don Angelo thought.

His thoughts continued. *He had to have. I now want the both of them!*

Don Angelo ordered a few of his men to go out and look for Mickey. The soldiers in particular, who were familiar with how he looked. The mob leader wanted him alive rather than dead. He had a few questions for Mickey before having him whacked. But truthfully, what the Don failed to realize was that Methuselah "Mickey" Savage, was a budding Don himself in his own right. And not only that. Mickey possesses absolute thinking abilities, to potentially have something drastic done against Don Angelo, before he could have him touched. Whether by cross-out with the police involved, or by dropping a contract on his head, with some brazen hardcore, nothing to lose Philly hitter from Black Mafia Incorporated. Mickey had options.

The situation now became a "dog-eat-dog" like scenario, that may have no end in sight. People were subject to die in the process. That was only if Don Angelo chose to act irrationally, rather than in a logical fashion like he always had. The challenge was on.

Chapter 13

The engagement phase for Josephine and Winston was flowing smoothly and according to plan. They were looking to speed up the process on the specific thing that they were looking to do, have a baby and get married. Or, if able to get Mickey to divorce her sooner, get married then have a baby. Whichever one was to happen first.

JoJo stopped taking those birth control pills like she told Winston she would, and the two were going at it like crazy, having unprotected sex in their efforts to conceive.

Josephine was so caught up with the good life she now lived and preoccupied trying to please Winston, that she overlooked an issue that was beginning to take root right under her nose. This was something so serious and so traumatizing that it could cause a long degree of harm, if the wrong continued to go unchecked.

The problem was that Winston found himself beginning to look at JoJo's eldest daughter Mary, with a wanton eye. This would happen anytime he was home alone with the kids and JoJo was away. These were the days he had duty to get them from school throughout the weekend and some days over the weekend.

Mary was only seven at the time and had no understanding regarding an inappropriate touch on her body from one that wasn't. Winston would undress the little girl in preparation to take a bath by herself, and he would deliberately run his hands firmly over her buttocks, legs, and privacy. He would then lift her to be placed into the tub. Not by her waist or under the armpits. But, by his hands locked around her thighs, palming her by her buttocks in this way.

The more time with the kids Winston had, the more aggressive he got with little Mary in his perversions. Winston became a sick man. JoJo didn't have a clue of what her husband to be was doing to her daughter, not to mention, the next phase of their relationship inadvertently blinding her more.

"Winston! Baby! I'm pregnant," JoJo announced. She was so excited.

Prior to the day, JoJo visited the doctor's office being that she'd missed her cycle and had not been feeling so well.

"You are! Baby, that's awesome! I've never had so much joy before in my life. How did you find out?" Winston responded.

"I'm a mother of five, babe. I know when I'm with child," JoJo said.

"That's understandable. But I hope we have a son together, so I can name him after me. But if we end up having a girl, then we'll have to come up with a beautiful name together."

"Sounds fantastic to me."

"Now about the other part we need to finally get situated. The divorce from the guy you're currently bound to. God knows that this needs to happen soon. As fast as we can make it happen," stated Winston.

"Yes … it does. But I know I can't go to him talking about a divorce while I'm a pregnant woman. I don't need the stress or the frustration while I'm carrying this baby. That won't be healthy. So, I think we need to wait it out to approach him, until I have the baby. If that's ok with you?" she requested.

Winston thought over all she'd said before offering a response. "Ok, hun. That's not a problem because I want for you and my baby to be as healthy as could be. Therefore, we wait. But in the meantime, I want to plan a trip for us. Let's visit my family in France. Just you and I. We can leave the kids with a nanny here. Or, we can have your sister keep them for us. The one who lives in New Jersey you speak so highly of. Besides, it's the summer. School has just let out. And I'm sure that they want to enjoy their time out."

Winston did his best to encourage JoJo to see things his way. It worked.

"Winston, I'd love that for us. I have always wanted to visit another country. And in particular, France. I'm so in love with French culture. Especially the type of mannerisms that they have, and the artists who paint or write. But once we're there, maybe we could make sweet love under the Eiffel Tower, skinny dip in the Seine River, and enjoy endless varieties of crepes for breakfast while in bed naked, baby! Yes! Take me! I'm so ready to go!" JoJo let out ecstatically.

She had more to say. "I'll be sure to contact my sister Natalie and have her drive here to get the kids. That'll be the opportunity I've long wanted to introduce you to her. And once that happens, off to Paris we go. I'm ready to sip wine and romance the entire time we're to be there."

"Absolutely, babe. We're on our way," he responded.

The two took the conversation from there directly to the act of foreplay. They made love as never before. Winston was sure to promise JoJo many things. The more he filled her head with the multitude of fantasies he had, the farther removed from the independence she once held onto. This was the direction in life Winston wanted her to go, to be a servant in a sense, under his dictation, and doing all that he said to do. Winston was becoming a master at manipulation. And JoJo the puppet to the puppet-master, doing the very things he pulls the strings for her to do. If only she recognized.

***

Dolan Estafan, Tracy's father, and a made man in the ranks of the Marconi crime family, went to Don Angelo to report that he had a missing daughter, and she hadn't been seen nor heard from in a couple of weeks. Something wasn't right, and Dolan knew it. This wasn't like Theresa to do such a thing.

To begin the conversation with Don Angelo, Dolan was immediately instructed not to make any type of report to the police, due to the type of risk that was involved. It could potentially open the door for investigation into many other things. Dolan was instead told to trust and rely upon the help of the Philly police officers who were already on payroll. But there was only so much that the paid cops could do. And this would lead to the Marconi men taking matters into their own hands, in order that justice be had. The type of justice that they wanted.

While at his home before going to Don Angelo, Dolan did a search in his daughter's bedroom. He stumbled upon her diary and an address book she had. These were interesting discoveries for Dolan, because they contained the contact information of all the people Theresa was most in touch with. Of them all, there was listed a boyfriend she absolutely adored. The name "handsome Nimble Neil" was how Theresa entered his name. Dolan had no idea about the daughter's boyfriend already being a marked man by the mob he was a part of. He was to be made aware in due time.

Along with his concerns, Dolan took the books he found to Don Angelo as well. There were a few men already in the presence of the Don when Dolan arrived. Don Angelo excused them all so as to have a private moment with him.

Dolan handed over the address book but only made mention of the diary. It was too personal. And also, Dolan maintained the thought that his daughter may eventually show up again at some point soon, then, he could hand her back her property.

Once informed about the affair between Theresa and Neil, Don Angelo came at Dolan with a hard line of questions.

"Dolan, do you have any knowledge of this Neil guy that your daughter was dating?" Don Angelo asked.

"Not at all, Don, not in the least," Dolan responded.

"So, you've never seen him or anything, I am to assume?"

"No sir, Don."

Don Angelo pondered deeply on what questions he might be able to ask next.

"Do you have any idea how long your daughter may have been dating this guy we now speak of? This Neil character?"

"According to the address book and her diary, the two have dated for over a year now."

The Don pondered further. He had his left hand situated on his chin, cupping it with the index finger and thumb. The robbery and lost product was now heavily on his mind. He now had a quest which may put him closer to solving both problems he had.

"Let me ask you, Dolan. You ever taken your daughter with you to either pick-up my brother, or to deliver him home?"

"I have, Don. On a few occasions. Why is it that you ask?" Dolan replied.

Don Angelo looked on at him sternly, as if to clearly imply that he's the one who does all the questioning. Not have it the other way around. Dolan understood the silent message conveyed. The Don then proceeded.

"Has Peter and you done any talking about business in your daughter's presence?"

"We may have, I don't recall right off."

"What about transporting any material ... any product ... while she rode along?"

"Again Don, we may have. I don't recall. However, when I bought her a car of her own, I stopped driving her to work or picking her up. No more trips around town either," Dolan confirmed.

The Don had a thought to himself. The damage may have already been done by then.

Whether Dolan's daughter Theresa knew it or not, she'd unintentionally exposed the business of the family to Neil through general conversations they would have and the style of questions he asked. Through it all, Neil was able to put it all together and make sense of it, to make the robbery go smoothly like it had. If it was one thing Neil was really good at, that was his craft of speculating and figuring things out. Speculation was his specialty.

Dolan spoke out once more before Don Angelo was able to ask more questions.

"But Don Angelo, my baby-girl, had never seen any of the products that we transported. Either to or from the underboss's home. And, she had no knowledge of any of the business," stated Dolan, the six-two, nearly three-hundred-pound hairy Italian sloth. He would put you in the mind of an ungroomed Alfred Hitchcock with a stubble beard, or a Bobby from *The Sopranos* before Bobby from *The Sopranos*.

"I never made any accusations, Dolan. The problem that we face is, some guy who goes by the name 'Nimble Neil'— more than like the same one you have become aware of that was dating your daughter—has presented a problem for this family. He belongs to Scalia. A rival. And, we may have been compromised by him in another way. Things have transpired I can't tell you of. Not at this time. Nonetheless, I need for you to make it your life's business to locate this Neil individual and bring him to me. I want your search for him to be as if your life depended upon you finding him. I want him here, on the floor at my feet. Half-alive if you have to. Just alive. I need to have a word or two with him. And in the meantime, I am going to have to suspend you from your driving detail for a time being and from security. From this family for that matter! At least until you get me Neil, or, until other developments clear up the many things not known at this particular time. Am I understood on this?" Don Angelo ordered, cuffing tightly the address book at the same time.

Dolan gave a hard look at Don Angelo. He was astonished at everything last ordered by his leader. He couldn't believe what had just taken place. To him, it was as if Don Angelo was blaming him and his daughter for something. Not to mention the fact that Dolan went to him in hurt and emotional pain, because his daughter was missing, and was possibly dead. That her boyfriend might have kidnapped her and done something to the girl. Don Angelo seemed to purposely overlook what Dolan came to him about and put his heroin business above that of Dolan's daughter's life.

Opposite Don Angelo not mentioning anything to Dolan about the robbery and taking of the product and cash, Peter had already revealed everything to Dolan. Dolan felt some type of way behind Don Angelo holding back specifics and casting blame over going about the investigation in a more proper fashion.

Dolan's salty attitude, held damaging to Dolan more than anything, was the impression that Don Angelo left upon the man with his specific finger-pointing questions. Dolan began to feel in the moment, like it may be Don Angelo, who had his daughter kidnapped and killed. Her car was towed and impounded, leaving him to be the one to go and get it back. Dolan knew that whatever happened to Theresa took place while she was at work or on the way home from work. And not too many people knew where the girl worked, other than a few of his mafia brethren. Don Angelo included. Dolan now had a beef with his leader.

Dolan responded to Don Angelo. "Yes, Don, you're understood," he lastly said, then walked out his presence. He had many things on his mind that needed to be sorted out.

Dolan began to think that his many years of loyalty, blood, sweat, and tears to the Marconi family stood for nothing at that point to Don Angelo. And his trust in the Don faded. He felt betrayed. And the degree of which he felt betrayed, made it to where there could be no reconciliation. The man's daughter was missing and believed to be dead. And in Dolan's mind now, Don Angelo ordered the hit. Why else would he push him away from the family? So, there could be no form of retaliation on Dolan's part, and the Don and his brother were safe from potential harm. These actions perpetrated against Dolan was the straw that broke the camel's back. And he was now eager to take action.

***

Ever since the day Neil and Theresa first met, she had no serious knowledge of how involved he was with the Scalia crime family. Her only objective was to find love and be loved, in a special way. Neil provided this for her, and the two had beautiful chemistry. Maybe he had good intentions to begin with. Maybe not. But the more and more Theresa opened up to him and revealed the activities she knew her father participated in—who he drove for and held security over, and the type of conversations that the father and underboss Peter Marconi would have—the temptation to put together a scheme to take from him simply became too irresistible to pass up. He had a lot to benefit by supplying someone who was brave enough to pull off the caper.

Fortunately for him, he had a bold and fearless associate he was able to tap to do the job. He was a crazy motherfucker who went by the name "Hound Savage," a hardcore street nigga who'd earned his stripes hunting down who or what he wanted, to take down or kill. This was the perfect fool and a psycho for the work he had in mind, so thought Neil.

Neil outsmarted Tracy. He lied to her by claiming to be in the business of selling insurance policies. He'd claimed to need all the addresses Peter Marconi had on file, to mail him brochures and other special offer presentations, that Peter was a potential client. Neil even went so far as to pay Theresa for the information he sought. She fell headfirst to the ploy.

Not only did Theresa provide the primary home address. She provided that of the game room in south Philly too. It was in Peter's name, and a few other properties owned by the underboss. Theresa also had personal knowledge on how to get to Peter's home. Through it all, she'd been used and deserted by Neil, leaving her as only being a means to an end. He played her like a fiddle and made no qualms to himself in doing so. Theresa and her family would pay the price behind the dirty deed. Love would get you each and every time.

Chapter 14

In The Meantime...

Johnny Mack had the duty yet again, to hold down the fort of the Savage family's empire that they were building while Mickey was away down south. He and Miss Peaches were looking to get back at Bobby Kavanaugh. And in a serious way.

Hound was available to assist Johnny Mack, but at the same time he wasn't, due in part to him branching out and doing his own thing with the large quantity of product he had. Black Mafia had numbers and territory now and was looking to expand and gain more strength. They were putting down the press and muscle on others. Hound was one of the top leaders.

Mickey had it in mind to convince as many male family members there in Georgia, to relocate to the north in Philly, to either join the fold in the streets with he, Johnny Mack, and Hound, or to go the legit route and start a business or something to the effect of. The construction and brick masonry sector of the City of Brotherly Love, really, began to boom around this time, and Mickey's people knew how to perform this type of work. The Savage family was a large and viable clan of folks. They had talents that could be exploited for the benefit of the family as a whole. Mickey knew exactly how to work it out.

Meanwhile, Johnny Mack wanted to have a word with Hound. He contacted him and asked him to come over to

Jersey for them to do so. Natalie was away visiting JoJo. The two would have the privacy to visit JoJo. The two would have the privacy to talk as they saw fit.

***

Hound made the drive across the Ben Franklin Bridge to his cousin's home.

"What's up, Johnny Mack? I'm here. What's on that busy mind of yours these days?" Hound greeted once let inside. The two slapped fives and embraced with a hug.

"And where that wife and those bad-ass kids of yours? I ain't seen them in a while. They is family," Hound continued.

"I'm glad you was able to make it, Hound. My wife and kids are away. They went to visit JoJo and her kids. Mickey's family. Wherever they live now. But that's another story for another day. I don't care to get into it about that right now," Johnny Mack responded. He took notice of the concerned look Hound had at the mention of the situation between Mickey and his wife. Hound only had little knowledge about the separation.

"Their business ain't our business," Johnny Mack further stated.

"I know that to be the truth. But what was it you wanted to speak to me about?" Hound asked.

"The future business between the three of us, me, you, and Mickey. Now that we know the full story behind your come up, what the hell are we supposed to do about supply once we all run out and you ain't got nothing left to sell us again? We can't go back to Angelo for more, I wouldn't assume. Don't know what he may know by now. And we can't allow ourselves to walk into a trap, no kind of way. And we ain't got a new dealer to supply us dope. So, what's the next move? The both of us need to figure this out here and now, that way, once Mickey gets back, we'll already have the game plan laid out and rolling," Johnny Mack stated.

"Well, for one, if the guineas eventually come to learn anything about who did what, which I'm sure they may, we won't have a choice but to eliminate the threat, if and when it comes our way. Besides, I got enough Black Mafia hitters on my hands, to go bonkers when I say so! Them Italian mofos don't want it with us! Because we coming with nothing but heat, blowing away any would be problems we may have. It's that simple," declared Hound, with a serious tone to his voice and expressive demeanor.

"Just like that, Hound!" Johnny Mack remarked.

"Just like that!" Hound retorted. "Now about product. I'm more than sure we could easily go to New York, and find somebody to sell us H. Some heavy dealer named 'Bumpy Johnson,' been creating a lot of waves lately. From what I've been told, he's established. A few people from the crew go to the Big Apple on the regular to shop for clothes. They get all the news on what's happening in the streets while there. So, to answer your questions, we keep shit moving like that. And, if I so happened to be killed in the process, or go back to prison, then y'all keep shit moving. Or vice versa," Hound expressed his realistic perspective.

Johnny Mack took a long pause to think over all Hound emphatically stated. By his own admission, Johnny Mack knew that his cousin Hound had become a certified live wire. He was now a goon who was death-struck to the core. The only question to remain was, how long would he live? Or, how far was he willing to go?

Johnny Mack came to the conclusion that he needed to do the necessary and get inside Hound's mind, so as to control the beasts that be. Hound was of good use to the family in so many ways, and if only somebody had the ability to contain him and make some sense to him—or manipulate him even, in this regard—he'd be able to keep his mind focused on the big picture and his guns aimed in the direction to keep enemies away. But truth be, Johnny Mack and Mickey had the mental sway to control the lunatic they had in Hound, to not do more crazy shit. He always listened to those two.

The conversation continued.

"Okay so, that part there, we good on ... knowing which direction we are to go to re-up on supply," Johnny Mack said. "Now, on to something else."

"And that is?" Hound responded. His interest always perked at new prospects.

"We need a sure shot. Someone to do a big job. That nigga you got on the team you mentioned who had one. The cat who sold us the guns we got."

"Frank. You talking about my guy Frank?"

"Yeah! Him! How certain is his shot?"

"I'd bet my life on it," Hound stated with confidence. "He was an official marksman in the military."

"That's all I need to know. We may need him to help us out with something. That way, we can get back to living like we want to, without fear of our past. And I'm the one putting this together. Mickey will get filled in later down the line at some point. Because for some reason, his plan to deal with this shit, seems to continue to go to hell with gasoline draws on! But the one I got in mind, will send somebody else there, and finally free us of the burden that hangs over our heads," Johnny Mack explained.

"Damn! That type of party, huh!" Hound responded.

"You damn skippy, it is! So be sure to run it by Frank, that he got a job on deck in that area in due time. And to be ready when I call on him."

"Will do. But in the meantime. I got about eight kilos left. Y'all want 'em?"

The two continued in conversation. Johnny Mack was sure to reveal a lot to Hound that was to go into the plot. He was a determined man to end the problem once and for all.

Chapter 15

Meanwhile,
Down South in Georgia...

"Chatham County District Attorney's office! How may I help you?" the secretary answered. A call came through from a specific person.

"Yes, this is Evelyn Ayton. I would like to speak with Robert Kavanaugh, please. I need him to know that I finally gave birth to our son," stated Miss Peaches in response. The sabotage campaign launched by Mickey and her had begun.

"Ma'am, if you're needing to speak with the D.A., then I can put you through. However, personal business isn't my area."

"I said it how I wanted you to receive it. But yes, please put me through to him. He and I need to talk."

"One moment please," the secretary lastly stated then put the phone on hold.

Nearly a minute later, Bobby took the call.

"D.A. Kavanaugh here! How may I help you?" he said, already knowing that Peaches was on the other line, but trying to downplay things.

"Bobby! You nasty, low down, dirty son of a bitch, you!" she spat.

"Evelyn! What on God's green earth do you want? And why did you call this office?"

"Muthafucka'! You tried to kill me. I'll never forgive you! And now, I promise you everybody is gonna know that you had a baby by another outside your marriage! Have you taken the time to have a look at the newspaper lately? If you haven't, you should. I plan to make everybody I can, aware of us. And I kept all the receipts to where we stayed together to help prove it," she informed. Her and Mickey made it their business to place ads in the newspaper for a month long-term, to announce the birth of the baby of Peaches and Bobby. A photo was included as well.

"Evelyn! You did what?" Bobby responded. He became livid.

"You heard me clearly. Ain't no need to repeat myself. And I look forward to going to court to have you pay up to support our baby. I'm sure once that wife of yours finds out about this, she'll divorce you, muthafucka'! Now, what you gotta say for yourself?"

"Evelyn, I'm hanging up this phone, ok? And if you continue to keep up this craziness, I'mma have a judge sign off on an order, and we'll see to it that you be put away in the psych ward in Milledgeville. Now don't push my patience, darling. Bye!" Bobby spat, then slammed the phone down on the hook in a fit of anger.

Miss Peaches called yet again. The secretary answered once more and put Peaches through to Bobby's line for another round of arguments.

"Evelyn, if you call this office one more time, I won't have no choice but to have a warrant taken out on you for harassing phone calls. Now quit it, ok?" he barked harshly.

"Go ahead, Bobby! Make my day. The more you try to push back and deny our affair and the baby we brought into this world, the better it will be for me. So, go on ahead. That's only more people who'll know. And not only that. I got a copy of your ID card and your social security card. I stole it from you the second time we were together while you were asleep. I was able to put it back once I did what I needed to do with it. You never noticed a thing. I plan to take you to court. So, no matter what, you are gonna acknowledge me and my baby, if that's the last thing you do. And I'm taking out an insurance policy in both our names for little Robert Francis Kavanaugh the second. I named him right after you, in the hospital down in Miami, away from Savannah. That way, you wasn't able to have somebody come and try to do something to one of us. How you love that! You bastard!" Peaches spat, then hung up the phone in a fit of anger.

"How was that?" Miss Peaches turns and asks Mickey.

"You did well, Now, onto the next part tomorrow. I need you to go down to the courthouse here and file a complaint to the court about Bobby abandoning his obligation to take care of his baby. More than likely, once you file the suit, the judge will subpoena you both to come before him, so as to get down to the bottom of the allegations. And that's gonna be the point when you tell everything about the affair. His wife will likely be there too, to hear it for herself. No doubt, she'll file for divorce, once the truth is out there. But, before you file the complaint, we will take out the insurance policy. It'll be a three-million-dollar policy to begin with, then we'll increase it from there. The point is to pressure Bobby to own up to everything. Or be forced to. The baby will be included into the main insurance policy Bobby has. And, included into the Kavanaugh estate as well. The judge will force it. And keep in mind, by the time the court hearing is scheduled, I will hire a lawyer to represent you. We definitely have to get one. I was thinking of one from out of Atlanta. The ones in this area are gonna be too afraid to go up against him. Just keep focused and not let anything he says intimidate you. Okay?" Mickey fully explained.

"I understand very well, Mickey. And like I said to you before, this better work. It can't fail. Okay? Please don't let this be a failure."

"It's gonna work. I promise it will. You'll have the law on your side. Working hard against the law. You won't be let down. I put my life on that," Mickey stated. He appeared very confident. This was something Miss Peaches needed out of him.

***

One Day Later...
Miss Peaches sprang into action doing all Mickey needed her to do. She went about doing things exactly how he needed her to, so as to leave no excuse why something had not worked.

Peaches took out the insurance policy first. Mickey put up the money through his father's namesake and the businesses they had established there in Savannah. She next made her way to the courthouse to file the civil complaint. Once that was complete, she made the last stop by the D.A.'s office to personally face Bobby, and to at least offer him the opportunity to see the son he'd help procreate, the son he'd always wanted. The hope with such a move was that he'd change his attitude.

Miss Peaches was fearful at first to approach Bobby personally again. But then, she came to the conclusion that there wasn't anything to be afraid of, because she had done nothing wrong. She suffered more from PTSD more than anything, as a result from the gunshot wound she was inflicted with. There was a need to overcome the anxiety associated, so as to move on how she felt needed to move on. The relief Peaches was looking for would come in due time.

Bobby came from the back-office area once made aware he had a visitor. He opened the door that led to the lobby and immediately took notice of his once lustful wonder, who was now holding a child. He was stunned beyond all his days at the sight of the two.

Miss Peaches was the first to speak out.

"One way or another, Bobby, you're gonna acknowledge me and this baby, and take responsibility like you're supposed to," she declared. Peaches showed him how serious she was with her presence.

"Evelyn Ayton!" he barks. Have you lost your ever-loving mind, gal! Huh! What business do you have showing up at my place of work! Now, you get! Or I'm calling the police!" he spat vehemently, stabbing a finger towards the door.

"So, you still wanna play this game, I see. Well, I've got one I can play too. It's called 'show and tell,' Bobby. Just the game I like to play, Bobby," Peaches responded, then pulled out a large legal envelope from the purse she carried and offered it to Bobby.

He took it from her and ripped it open, eager to know the content that was inside. Bobby was in for a huge surprise.

One-by-one, he pulled out the large 8 by 10-inch photos from the packet. They were of a smiling him and Miss Peaches on the beach in Miami, hugging and kissing throughout the series of pictures. She then pulled out a second envelope. These showed the two in the nude having sex in the hotel suite. They were taken from the ceiling above the bed, and showed his face looking upward, as he lay on his back. And finally, a third envelope with photos of the two at the Clay versus Liston heavyweight fight together.

Bobby's jaw dropped. His mouth flung open. His face became flush with a devil red color of blood. Man, was he pissed.

"Where in the hell did these come from!" he growled.

"From yours truly, me. And Mickey too, might I add. The ones you have there belong to you. We got extra copies. And just so you know… about an hour ago before I came here, I went over to the courthouse and filed a civil complaint against you for child negligence. A copy of a few of those photos was included. So, you really thought you were playing me, didn't you? But at the same time, Mickey was protecting me and playing you. And for me to think that you were as smart as I gave you credit for being, how wrong was I. All you had to do was the right thing and acknowledge me and our baby. But the problem you now have is one you created. Don't feel bad. Because I ain't know nothing about what Mickey was doing behind the scenes. He outsmarted us both but safeguarded me in the process. So, now my question to you is, do you plan to sing a different tune than you had before? The last one didn't sound too well. Maybe it will now, I believe," Peaches let out. Her response was long and cold. She had a snicker of laughter behind her words.

Bobby appeared more dumbfounded in that instance than he had in all his days of living. He was at a complete loss for words and had no idea of how to defend against the attack that was launched upon him.

With Mickey being the mind behind the plot, he had to be in possession of one hell of a forethought to gain the upper hand over Bobby in this way. He was several moves ahead. This had long been contemplated, before Bobby built up the balls to take aim and shoot at Mickey and Peaches.

What really gave Mickey the edge with the plan he had in mind was, he'd hired a private eye to keep a close watch on Bobby at any time he had Peaches to hook up with him. This was done to protect himself, in the event that either of the two was to conspire and try to kill him in a double-cross, then later ride off into the sunset together like nothing ever happened. Bobby and Miss Peaches, that is.

The investigator was set up inside the room of the hotel down in Miami next to the one Peaches stayed each time they went. This was the reason why Mickey always had Miss Peaches to have Bobby come to her, and never she to him. The private eye created access through the ceiling from one room to another. Above Peaches' room, he drilled tiny holes through the ceiling over the bed to set his camera lens there to take pictures from multiple angles, and snap away at any moment there was action. Mickey was determined as ever to not allow Bobby to frame him for the Maddox girl rape and murder and send him to prison behind it. Neither was he going to let Bobby cause him to take the fall for the disappearance of those two cops, Flaherty and Carson. And above all, he couldn't allow Bobby the chance to get the drop on him and either kill him personally or have him killed by someone else. Therefore, Mickey had to out-think him. And needed to do so at a high level.

Once stating all she needed to say, Miss Peaches stood to her feet, pulled back the small blanket from over the baby's head, and spoke her peace one last time for the day.

"If you were wondering, Bobby, here is what your son looks like. And consider this a courtesy, because it's the first and last time you'll ever see him again, if you continue to deny him. The choice is yours. It's all on you. So, bye!" she lastly stated, then stormed across the lobby floor and out the building.

Bobby immediately got on the phone, once back in his office and called the court. The clerk confirmed that indeed a suit had been filed, naming him as the defendant. He knew then that Peaches hadn't lied. That her trouble was real. He had to do something to stop the effect of her actions from working and snowballing out of control. His back was now against the wall, leaving him no longer the power figure in the affair he once had. It was Miss Peaches who was.

Chapter 16

While still down in Georgia, Mickey made it his business to take a ride to Eatonton, Georgia, to the home of JoJo's parents. He'd only been there once and knew the location. His intention was to check and be sure that JoJo hadn't moved back home. And if not, he would attempt at having the mother or father provide him with whatever current phone number that they had to her, as he only wanted to see his kids, and took what JoJo had done to him as a wrong. Mickey felt as though JoJo could have left him as she saw fit to do. But why would she not allow him anytime with his children? This was the part he was pissed about the most.

He knocked on the door. It was still early in the day. The mother hadn't long gotten home from work and was there alone.

"Mickey!" she let out once opening the door. "How you doing? It's been a long time. But I still remember you. What brings you here?" she asked a question that she already had the answers to.

"I'm doing pretty good. And I think the both of us already know why I'm here. I need to know if or not JoJo and my kids have been by, or was living back here in Georgia again? But, I see that they are not."

"Nope. they are not. We haven't seen her since you took her from us and y'all moved north. Haven't seen the grandkids either. All JoJo has done is call and allow us the chance to talk with them over the phone. Nothing more," the mother responded.

"Did she ever mention anything to you about the problems that we were going through?" Mickey asked.

"She did. I know about the two of you being separated. I'm aware she moved out. They live in New Hampshire now—"

"New Hampshire!" Mickey retorted. "Who in the hell JoJo knows there?"

"I have no clue. All I know is, she bought a house there."

"She took half my money from my safe when she left. So, that's how she was able to do that. I didn't have a problem with it because I know she spent it on my kids. And they got a good place to live. But what else?"

"Last I heard, JoJo got some white guy in her life now. They are engaged. He looking to marry her someday. But that can't happen at the—"

"Until she gets a divorce from me first," Mickey cut in to say.

"Yes. that. One other thing, Mickey. JoJo's pregnant. By him. The white guy."

Mickey looked at the mother with a disgusted demeanor about his face. He was stunned to know JoJo would do such a thing. Of all JoJo had said or done that he took as a disrespect, this one hurt the most. He felt as if his soul had been pierced.

"You can't be for real, are you! How could she! I know we got a few issues to work out in what we have. Or shall I say what we had. But JoJo couldn't allow herself to wait until we took care of our business, before she decided to go off and make a baby with somebody else?" Mickey let out and continued to shake his head in disbelief at the news of his wife.

"I guess not, Mickey. Life has to still go on no matter what," the mother stated.

"I guess it does, doesn't it? But anyway, you take care now, okay?" Mickey lastly said then stepped away. He got into the car and drove away. He wasn't angry or anything of that nature. Only at a loss for words.

Mickey returned to Savannah. He and Miss Peaches shared a hotel suite together. Sparkle stayed behind in Philly. She and Peaches had a home together there.

Peaches took her baby to her mother's house. She and Mickey had additional business to handle for the remainder of the time they were to be in Georgia and needed to continue in their progress in an undetected way. Although Mickey wasn't a wanted man behind anything, there was still a need to play it safe in going up against Bobby Kavanaugh, as past history proved. But, little did Mickey know, Johnny Mack was the more active of the two, with putting together a plot, to free them both from the ill-deed they'd committed in 1958. This particular plot would permanently clear them of any issue the blood-thirsty and ambitious D.A. may have had in mind to settle with them. Johnny Mack now only needed to see to it that it happened.

***

Two Weeks Later...

Mickey and Miss Peaches were back in Philly. Before leaving Georgia, he was sure to hire a lawyer like he said he'd do, to represent her. The lawyer would definitely see to it that the suit filed against Bobby, be properly channeled through the court. Mickey also demanded from the lawyer that he keep him informed of the fallout with the public Bobby was sure to have, and the filing for divorce that Bobby's wife would no doubt submit to the court. Bobby's career as a prosecutor was destined to experience a devastating downfall.

Mickey would begin getting the phone calls from the lawyer to inform, faster than he originally anticipated. The effects of their work occurred dramatically.

Chapter 17

In The Meantime...

Joey and his crew of mafia soldiers were able to track down the Nimble Neil guy they'd been looking for. He was out in Pittsburgh as they'd been informed he'd be. The contact information inside the address book Theresa had turned out correct. This was a smart move on Don Angelo's behalf to keep the book when Tracy's father presented it to him.

The Marconi henchmen took Neil hostage, tied him tightly with duct tape, gagged him with a ripped tee shirt, then hauled the marked man back to Philly locked inside a casket and driven in a hearse. This was the perfect cover up for a dead man who happened to still be breathing. But only for a short time longer. Don Angelo had a few things he wanted to drill the guy about before he was to have him meet his horrible fate. This was to be literally and figuratively.

Joey arrived at the designated location he was told to be. It was a home in northeast Philly. Don Angelo and his team of executors were already there awaiting.

He pulled into the garage. The door to it was lowered once again. All of Don Angelo's men brought out the casket, and Joey popped open the top lid to it. There lie poor Neil, eyes bucked wide, half curled in the fetal position and terrified out of his mind.

They yanked him from the casket and dragged him across the rough concrete floor to a metal seat bolted to the floor.

Neil was then shackled and cuffed to a bar that extended from there.

Don Angelo was a leader of very few words. He was a pointed man and a straight shooter when it came to getting down to the bottom of a problem or resolving one.

Joey took the gag from Neil's mouth and allowed him the opportunity to speak up when spoken to once Don Angelo began.

"Nimble Neil, they call you, huh?" Don Angelo let out in a calm low tone of voice. "I've been waiting to lay eyes on you for the longest. I believe we have some business to discuss."

"Yeah, I'm Neil. And who are you? Why am I here?" Neil responded. He maintained a sense of respect while speaking to an elder. He also quickly recognized that the old man, whoever he was, called the shots.

"Who am I, you ask? I'm Angelo. 'Don Angelo Marconi' that is. And, if you belong to the Scalia family, I'm sure you've heard of me. My brother Peter as well. His home was the one you and your black criminal friend robbed and took my narcotic product from. Don't ask me how I know. Just know that I know. And I'd like to hear from you, all about that. So, what do you have to say for yourself? We have you all alone. And no one could help you. However, you do have the opportunity to help yourself. Now talk," Don Angelo emphatically stated.

"Mister Angelo … I'mma be straight up with you on this one, ok? I had nothing to do with any of it. I'm an innocent man of what you have accused. It wasn't my call. And it wasn't my doing," Neil responded. He was aiming to lie his way out of the situation.

"So, you mean to tell me, you have no clue who Estefan is? You have no knowledge of where my brother lived? And you didn't receive any cut from the product that was taken from me?" Don Angelo laid out a strong series of questions.

"Absolutely not, Mister Angelo. How would I know where your brother lived? And how would I know he had heroin stashed in his home? I know nothing about any of that, sir." Neil let out too much in that one exchange.

Don Angelo and Joey had a serious look at each other and smiled. They both knew then and there that Neil was lying like all hell.

Don Angelo continued, "So, not only are you a liar, you actually know how to tell the truth as well, since you were willing to make a confession on yourself in the way you have. Who other than you, mentioned anything about heroin being stashed anywhere?" he stated, revealing to Neil the incriminating words he'd spoken.

Don Angelo gave a nod of the head to the stocky one of the goombah soldiers. That was code for, "do work." To inflict pain.

The loyal henchman swaggered from his position towards Neil. He had a power-drill in his hands. There was a thick seven-inch bit attached to it. The cord was uncoiled and dragged along behind him. Joey took the pleasure of plugging it into the electric box. The goon with the power tool, stood directly in front of Neil and smiled at him. He raised the drill like a pistol and pointed the tip at him. He then pulled the trigger to it, causing the bit to twirl terrifyingly. Suddenly, the goon speared the bit into the top of Neil's right knee and held the trigger to it. Neil howled to the moon and back from the amount of pain he felt. He panted and gasped for air. Shock had nearly set in. The goon withdrew the tip and awaited the command to do so once more.

"You want to speak the truth now? Or do my soldiers here need to give you more pain?" stated Don Angelo. He played the tape recording of Lacy's last words at that point. Neil's name was clearly mentioned.

Don Angelo was sure to bring up all he knew about the affair that went on between Neil and Tracy. The information that the address book had inside it. Neil couldn't deny any of it. He began to forge another lie, so as to try and take some of the blame from himself.

"Ok! Look!" he let out, clearly in obvious pain. "The girl's father, Mister Angelo! Dolan! That's his name, right?"

"What about the girl's father?" Don Angelo responded.

"Him! He's the one who provided me with the information about Peter and the drugs he had stashed at his home. Eighty kilos it was, right? How else would a 'Scalia' guy like me know about anything a 'Marconi' underboss got goin on, if someone on the inside didn't let me know? Now, there you have it. So, free me! Because if you don't, a mafia war between our two families will soon begin. And you, Don Angelo, don't really want that. Because that'll make you the one responsible for breaking the peace treaty that's in place to prevent a war. Now, wouldn't it?" Neil stated. He was still experiencing a lot of pain.

Don Angelo looked at Joey once more, cocked his head to the left and shrugged his shoulders. He appeared not to give a shit at that point. So much for peace. The war had already started.

"So, as it is … so, shall it be!" spat Don Angelo, then gave the order to the executioner to terminate the treacherous weasel without fail.

The henchmen pulled the trigger to the drill yet again, giving life to it. He rammed the tip of the fast-twirling bit directly between Neil's eyes, penetrating the skull and winding his brain in the process. Neil's shout for help didn't last long. His death came fast and cruel. He was no more.

With the main person behind the plot eliminated, it was time for Don Angelo and his team of loyal mobsters to move on to get the next, then the next, and whosoever else that may have had a hand in the robbery and thievery of his dope. He was a furious man.

Chapter 18

Johnny Mack called Mickey and asked him to stop by his place the very first chance he was available. That there was an important situation going on, and it required them to meet in person. He claimed to have a huge surprise for Mickey, and he needed to hurry and get there.

Mickey wasted no time taking the short drive across the river to New Jersey. Once there at Johnny Mack's house, hopped out of his car and damn near ran to the front door in a fit of anxiousness to know what Johnny Mack had that was so important to show him. Johnny Mack met Mickey at the door, opened it, and let him inside.

Mickey looked Johnny Mack directly in the eyes. He was met only by a loving smile the cousin had to offer.

"What's the urgency, nigga?" Mickey demanded to know.

"Calm down, Methuselah! Damn, nigga! It's serious, but not that type of serious!" Johnny Mack responded.

Natalie heard them both in the living room. She appeared from the kitchen, took a look at Mickey to know that it was indeed his voice she heard, turned up her nose at him, then returned to the kitchen to continue cooking.

"Well, what the hell is it, nigga?" Mickey demanded to know once more.

"Your kids are here, fool! They upstairs now! So, calm your ass down, nigga! You panic too goddamn much!" Johnny Mack stated with a smile. He caused Mickey to do the same.

"Hey, y'all bad-ass kids!" Johnny Mack yelled out. "Y'all daddy down here!" There were only four of them. The oldest, Mary, was sent to stay with Sasha until JoJo and Winston were to return from France.

Mickey felt really good to have the chance to spend time with his kids. He wanted to see the five of them, but after learning Mary's whereabouts, he knew she was A-ok, and became content with being there with the four behind her. They were just as happy to see him as he was them.

Johnny Mack let Mickey know how long the kids was supposed to be there with him and his wife and kids and told Mickey that it was ok to take his kids with him for the time being, on the promise he'd have them back before JoJo got home and wouldn't try to keep them from her. Mickey agreed. But truthfully, Johnny Mack didn't have to say a word to him and could've easily continued on letting Mickey stay in the blind. However, he felt he would have been wrong for not letting the man see his children and wouldn't be able to live with himself by not doing right by his own flesh and blood.

***

Mickey took his babies to Philly with him. He introduced them to Miss Peaches and Sparkle and explained who the two women were to him. Women friends he'd known for a while now. Sparkle had no kids. And due to the type of relationship that she and Mickey had, she immediately took it upon herself to treat them as if they were her own. Maybe someday, she and Mickey might be fortunate enough to have kids themselves. But, for the time being, Mickey and JoJo's kids were essentially hers too. No doubt about that.

The kids told their daddy and his girlfriend how life was for them in New Hampshire. He had so many questions for them. Probably more than they wanted to answer.

Nonetheless, they spoke truthfully to each one Mickey asked.

Chapter 19

Meanwhile...

Don Angelo now had two additional people on his hit list that he and his mobster goons were aiming to track down, that was Dolan Estafan, one of their own who was no longer able to be located, and Hound Savage, a name they'd heard one too many times, but weren't able to put a face to it. Also, someone who Don Angelo was for certain, had relations to Mickey Savage, due to Mickey no longer being able to be contacted, and him having the same surname as the intended target they were looking for.

Little to Don Angelo's knowledge, Dolan had a lot of influence throughout the ranks of the Marconi crime family. Dude was one hungry, ambitious, and effective mobster, who was driven by the pursuit of power, money, and a desire to lead how he saw fit in the future to come. At all costs, Dolan had a serious mind to be the boss and hold the top spot as such. Even if that meant to clip any and everybody who was in his path on the way up.

As far as Dolan knew, Don Angelo was the responsible one behind his daughter's kidnapping and death. He concluded that since she had not returned home or called, she had to be dead. Vengeance was a must. His mind, body, and spirit was set on taking action. Nothing could cause him to think or feel otherwise.

Throughout the days after the confrontation between he and Don Angelo, Dolan became active in recruiting a team of unhappy low-ranking individuals who lined the ranks of the family. He was sure to repeatedly remind them of all the laws and policies put in place by Don Angelo, that was in place to harm them or to hold them back: The heavy increase in monthly dues they had to pay, along with all the restrictions Don Angelo had in place to hinder them from the money making schemes they were not allowed to take part in. The young bucks had had enough with their greedy, old-fashioned, ineffective and grumpy leader they had in Don Angelo Marconi. Not to mention how he wanted them to be weak and soft-spoken at any time that they were in his presence. The bottom-line point that Dolan made for them became something to build a new foundation up. Don Angelo Marconi was no more useful and had to go. That was all there was to it.

Don Angelo had no idea at how bad the dislike for him was with the soldiers he had. One never knows until it's too late to know. And as for Don Angelo, it appeared too late. Or was it?

Mickey and Hound had gotten word from a reliable Italian source, someone who was close to Dolan and Rocco, that Don Angelo was in the process of putting a top-dollar hit on their heads, if the loyal Marconi soldiers didn't get to them first, and that the best thing for them to do was to have a sit down with him, and get down to the bottom of the shit pile, to clear their names. No doubt, they were willing to do so, but only under one condition. That the meeting takes place at a neutral location, and in a public space over a meal.

Mickey knew that no matter how crazy or chaotic that the most vehement of mafia men could be, none of them was stupid enough to open fire in an upscale public restaurant, attempting to kill someone. Especially not a crowded restaurant, something like that just didn't happen.

Don Angelo agreed when Mickey finally got in touch with him. He wanted to have a five-star steak dinner at one of the top spots in downtown Philly of the day, then he and the Savage boys could mull over who, when, what, how, and why as they enjoyed their meal. The expense was to be on Mickey, so said Don Angelo.

***

Days Later...

The day of the sit down was upon them. It was on a Thursday evening, the last week in July. The time was originally set for 6:00 p.m., but was eventually pushed back to 9:00, due to Don Angelo not liking to be out and about in public during the daylight hours. He feared that the busy FBI agents could easily snap photos of him and his men and document the movement and activities they might be involved in at any time.

Mickey was already in the habit of being properly dressed in business attire as Don Angelo would require, and as he was already accustomed to doing on a personal level. He and Hound arrived at the steakhouse that was located on Walnut Avenue and Broad Street then. They were forty-five minutes ahead of schedule, so as to scope out the place and ensure that they weren't being set up for an ambush. They rode in Mickey's Mustang. He parked at a distance down the block from the front entrance of the restaurant, on the same side. This was done to have a view of Don Angelo once they arrived, as he and his men would have to essentially pass by the two of them and not know it.

At five minutes to nine, Don Angelo's gleaming black Lincoln Continental eased past Mickey's Ford Mustang and pulled alongside the curb directly in front of the restaurant steakhouse. It rained all throughout the day. This became one of the main reasons also why the time to meet was pushed back. A drizzle still carried on. An umbrella or an ankle-length raincoat was required, in the event that a downpour began once more when the meeting was to start.

Both Mickey and Hound took notice of two other men in the car to accompany Don Angelo. Upon the Lincoln coming to a complete stop, the one in the back seat got out, popped open an umbrella and opened the door for Don Angelo to exit.

As Mickey and Hound stepped out of his car and made the trek towards the restaurant, they suddenly took notice of two men, both clad in long dark-colored raincoats, walking fast in the direction of Don Angelo, one on the opposite side of the street. It was too late for Mickey and Hound to turn and reverse course and not have any involvement in whatever it was that was about to go on. Their instincts kicked in to take action. Also, if anything was to be perpetrated against Don Angelo, they would be the ones to suffer the blame and then have the forces of the mafia and dirty cops on their heels gunning for them throughout the remainder of their lives. Something that they didn't need.

The two cousins had their pistols on them. They both carried automatics, .45 calibers.

"What the fuck!" Hound yelled out to Mickey as he observed the obvious. They were about thirty feet from Don Angelo's car.

"Don Angelo, watch out!" Mickey shouted.

Pow!

The attacker who was on the same side as was Don Angelo, fired the first shot.

Pow! Pow! Pow!

He let loose three more rounds, shattering the glass of the passenger-side door of the Lincoln. The gunmen both continued to walk towards Don Angelo's direction.

Pop! Pop! Pop!

The second shooter then began to fire away from his position across the street.

Boc! Boc! Boc!

Suddenly, a third shooter appeared, firing shots from behind Mickey and Hound, on the opposite side of the street.

He'd taken aim at Don Angelo as well. It was a hit on the life of the mafia leader unfolding then and there.

Mickey and Hound dropped low between the line of cars parked along the street. They had no choice but to withdraw their guns. Hound was amped and ready to roll, once they'd come to realize what was going on. He rose up to take a shot at the hitter who walked up from behind them.

Boom-Boom!

Hound struck him square in the head with one of the rounds he let off. The guy was about twenty feet over from him and Mickey. He never saw Hound from his side view. His focus was locked in on Don Angelo and the two men who were with him. Hound looked and took notice of the body dropping to the pavement.

"I got 'em!" Hound confirmed to Mickey.

Pow-Pow-Pow!

Pop! Pop-Pop!

The other two ambushers continued to fire away. Don Angelo's driver took a fatal shot to the face. His body fell forward with his head bumping against the steering wheel, pressing down on the horn. It blared constantly as the vicious melee dredged on.

Don Angelo was now perched low between the open passenger door of the car. The bodyguard who opened the door for him panicked and ran off from fear into the restaurant, essentially leaving the Don all to himself. Don Angelo made a desperate attempt to climb back into the Lincoln, only to find that his driver had been killed.

The two remaining assailants were now quickly closing in on Don Angelo. They were only a few feet away in front of him. And then …

Pow! Pow! Pow-Pow-Pow!

Boom-Boom-Boom-Boom-Boom-Boom-Boom!

Both Mickey and Hound made a short sprint towards Don Angelo's direction and began blasting with all they had with them to fight with. They effectively pushed the two shooters in a back-pedal, then eventually away and out of sight. They ran off. Mickey and Hound reached Don Angelo and properly secured him from further harm.

"Don Angelo! It's me, Mickey Savage! You ok? You not hit, are you?" he let out. "Hound! Here! Go get the car!" he yelled next, from the rush of adrenaline he experienced. He handed Hound the keys.

Hound ran off quickly.

Don Angelo was very disoriented and in a heavy state of delusion. He had somewhat blanked-out mentally and had no full idea of anything that took place throughout the entire two minutes or so of the gun battle.

"Don Angelo! It's me, Mickey!" he had to repeat, due to the mafia chief roving his head frantically from right to left, trying to come to terms with reality once more. Mickey continued. "Some guys just ambushed you and your men! They tried to assassinate you, Don Angelo! I'm gonna get you to safety, ok? But one of your men is dead!" he stated, looking on at the dead guy behind the steering wheel of the vehicle. The horn still blared away.

Hound now pulled up to the spot where Mickey waited with Don Angelo. The tires screeched as he jammed on the brakes to come to a stop. Opposite the volley of bullets no longer flying back and forth, Don Angelo was left with a gunshot wound to the shoulder he'd suffered. However, it wasn't life threatening. He would live to see another day. This would be enough time to make heads roll and bodies drop behind the failed hit on his life. There would be hell to pay for those who were responsible.

The Savage cousins rushed Don Angelo into the back seat of the Mustang, got in themselves, and hauled ass in the nick of time before the police were to arrive. There were two dead guys on the scene. One from each side. Not nearly enough explaining could be done to keep the police from making arrests, if anyone was to be caught on the scene.

Mickey had Hound drive them to his low-key home. This would allow Don Angelo the proper time to process it all and to rest for the moment if he felt the need to do so. Then afterwards, he could either have Mickey take him home, to one of his places of business in south Philly or, he could call his men to come pick him up. It didn't matter how he was to get to his next destination, the bottom line was, any beef or potential accusations Don Angelo had of Mickey or Hound Savage, they were now completely eliminated. The two literally had just saved the man's life. And he owed them a great debt of gratitude.

Mickey and Hound shouldn't ever run out of favors owed to them by Don Angelo. Their intention was to milk him thoroughly for all they could, and he would have to kiss their black asses if they wanted him to. This was how huge of a favor he owed. A debt he would never end paying so long as he was alive.

The Marconi Don would have to bow down and kneel to the Savage family gangstas' from there on out, rather he wanted to or not. There wasn't a choice. It was an obligation.

Chapter 20

Bobby Kavanaugh began to experience a stream of unfortunate occurrences behind the fallout and actions Miss Peaches put forth upon him. His decline from the high position he held as District Attorney began faster than Peaches and Mickey anticipated. His voter base and supporters, fled from him quicker than he could count to ten. The impending midterm elections were fast approaching. The forecast indicated an end result that Bobby didn't want to think about. Not to mention the lack of unity his office now had regarding the assistants who work for him. They deemed Bobby a hypocrite and an unethical misfit for the job. A plot was forming to force him to resign.

In addition to Bobby's career being in jeopardy, his personal life was unraveling and was made a public spectacle all about Savannah and the judicial circuit he worked in. The ongoing divorce made it this way. The wife had demanded he get out of the house. She had this leeway because both of their names were on the deed. He had no certain future regarding either of the two, work or home.

Bobby tried several times to get a warrant signed so as to have an arrest made on Mickey, in relation to the disappearance and possible death of the two policemen, Flaherty and Carson. However, each attempt failed. All the judges intown knew that Bobby had gotten it wrong in the past with the Norma Maddox case and didn't want their signature on a document that may prove to be wrong yet again. The thought was that Bobby sought to cast blame on someone else to cover for a nephew of his, and to the judicial officials of the law, it made not a difference if or not the man Bobby blamed was black. Justice was blind to them. She also had on a blindfold to cover her eyes.

There became a sense of urgency on Bobby's part to get proactive and do something of a drastic nature to Methuselah Savage. He reached out to an old friend of his. One who was familiar with Mickey himself. It was Jimmy Wilkens, aka "Pecan Slim." He'd made it to the rank of Captain on the police force and had a bone to pick with Mickey too.

The idea was for the two to collude with one another and make something stick on Mickey, for the old and the new. They intended to dig deep into the known activities of Mickey's past and charge him with something. Then suddenly, it dawned upon Bobby on how he could hit him below the belt, directly in the nuts. He remembered the story Miss Peaches told him of how young she was at the time she and Mickey became acquainted. And with that, it also came to the attention of Bobby that he was the one to have his niece forge the marriage documents for Mickey to make Josephine his wife. Bobby now wondered what the girl's actual age was in 1958.

Through it all, Bobby had something to work with to try and gain back an advantage over Mickey. Also, there was a guy by the name Otis Savage, who'd been recently arrested on the charge of "Felony Murder." He was Mickey's brother.

Otis and the man he killed, got into an argument over a gambling match. A poker game. The tongue wrangling turned into pistols being drawn and shots fired. Bobby had authority over the case. He could work a deal with Otis, only if Otis spoke on what he knew about Mickey, and his whereabouts at the time. Otis was dealt an ultimatum. Bobby had leverage once more.

***

JoJo and Winston had a pleasant time while in Paris, France. They really enjoyed their vacation. She had the opportunity to meet his family there and tour the city as no other tourist had. At least, in her mind that's how she felt. The food, the scenery, the love and romance that was in the air, the French culture—everything—was amazing to her. She could hardly wait to go back for a second time, as the promise to do so by Winston was given to her.

At home in New Hampshire, Winston began to press JoJo to do all necessary, to initiate the divorce process of her from Mickey. She swore to Winston that once their child was born, she would do all in her power to have Mickey sign off on the paperwork and free herself from being his wife. She and Winston could then be lawfully wedded as they desired at that point.

Atop of Winston demanding JoJo to rid herself legally from Mickey, he also felt the need to satisfy his inclination to know exactly how she and Mickey met, and what all their relationship involved? The thing he really wanted to know was, the story behind the sudden migration of the two from Georgia to the north, the part where JoJo seemed to always stop short on telling him. Emotion would overtake her. She was still terrified of even talking or thinking of it, of what could happen to her for failing to report the situation, as well play a part in why she separated herself and the kids from Mickey.

JoJo related the truth to Winston about the shooting itself but lied about being there at the time when Mickey pulled the trigger.

"So, this is why you and Methuselah up and leave from down south like that. At a time when you were pregnant and needed to be situated?" Winston responded to her revelations.

"Yes, Winston. This is why. I can't tell you exactly what happened in our house that awful night, because I wasn't home. Only my husband was. I went to my hometown to visit my parents and younger siblings. Me and Natalie. And what Mickey told me was that he and a cousin of his were running a 'speakeasy'—they bootleg moonshine—and the time approached closing. While they counted the money for the night, two men break down the door and barged in. Apparently, they were cops. Their intent was to bust them for illegal alcohol distribution. Mickey and the cousin assume the policemen to be dirty cops and were looking to extort them, because they didn't have on uniforms, and they'd fired the first shots. Mickey and the cousin shot back, killing the other two. This was the story he told me," JoJo said.

"What! Josephine! Are you serious?" Winston exclaimed.

"Yep. That's why I separated me and the kids from him. Because once the police finally do catch up to him, we won't be nowhere close by. And I won't have to face any consequences behind his actions."

"Josephine, you've got to hurry and get the divorce done so to completely be done and away from that guy. He's got problems. Big problems!"

"I know. And the divorce will happen soon. Just please, Winston. Let me have our baby first. And once I do that, then the other business will be taken care of. I don't need the stress of that while I'm pregnant."

"That's totally understandable, sweetheart. We just have to handle that so to live the life we desire to live."

"And we will. Once our baby is here."

The two then changed the subject and began to talk over other topics related to their relationship.

Little to JoJo's knowledge, Winston had other things in mind he wanted for his family. The very moment JoJo was to deliver their child, would be the instance the agenda he concealed in the darkness, would then come to the light. The man she thought she knew, held potential to be someone totally different from the person he always appeared to be.

JoJo would be forced to deal with each and every choice she'd made by choosing to be with Winston. If only life was simple as we made it out to be often times.

Chapter 21

Don Angelo Marconi was able to quickly get down to the bottom of the issue and learned who it was responsible for the failed hit on his life. It was Dolan, the once loyal and dedicated soldier who was a part of his family. Dolan was able to recruit the three henchmen he had to perform such a bold act against the mafia leader. One was a dissatisfied made man of Marconi's, while the other two were only associates. The police made a positive identification on the one that was coincidentally killed by Hound, with this information going public. He happened to be the lone made guy. The capo who the soldiers lined under was immediately demoted to a foot soldier once more by Don Angelo. He was deemed incapable of instilling strength in his unit of men to prevent being persuaded to commit treason. In all actuality, the capo was lucky to have walked away with his life. He was spared execution because Dolan was more to blame than anyone.

Don Angelo was sure to properly explain to his men the details of the assassination attempt. He also made them aware of who it was that was responsible for his still being alive. In addition to his revelations, he decreed that Mickey and Hound Savage, were now gracious friends of the family, and that absolutely no one would look upon them in the wrong way or think indifferently of the two at any time moving forward. This was an order. The Savage family was allowed to attend all social gatherings that the Marconi family hosted. There would be no reason to fear, nor would they receive any suspicious glances from anyone. If any of Don Angelo's men were to do otherwise, their actions would be met with a severe penalty.

Don Angelo's newfound way of how he felt of Mickey and Hound was because, not only had they risked their own lives to save his—they'd killed one of the men who was intending on killing him—the traitor from Marconi. They also had Don Angelo at their disposal to possibly do whatever harm to him they so pleased, or hold him hostage for ransom. But they treated him with proper care and respect. This turned out to be a triple victory for both sides. And because of this, Don Angelo had no choice but to chalk up any so-called beef that might have existed between the two groups.

The business relations resumed with Don Angelo providing both Mickey and Hound multiple kilos of his heroin product on consignment. The bond and friendship was solidified. The only thing of serious nature Mickey had left to do was to keep his crazy renegade cousin Hound, in his place and from putting them at risk again. That type of situation couldn't ever be a thing any more. It created a hostile and difficult predicament for the Savage enterprise, and on no level was that good for business.

Mickey and Hound would nonetheless prevail. And the understanding was that they needed not backtrack or fall off from that point moving forward. Their rise to power and influence in the underworld would continue. They were good to go. The only potential problem to this equation was that Hound still had the address book that was taken from Peter's home. It was jam packed with information on where Marconi mobsters had money making scheme operations. These were easy capers to pull off. And his itching desire to do so, couldn't be scratched to make him not go to that extreme.

Chapter 22

Josephine Savage and her Caucasian boyfriend, Winston Prather, received a knock at the door of their home. There was a group of men present. The ones that were never thought to appear. It was five members of the New Hampshire State Police, and two other men who accompanied the officers.

"May we help you?" Winston asked of the gang of seven as he and JoJo stood alongside one another.

"Yes, you may," stated the clean cut, casually dressed man who stood in the midst amongst the uniform officials. "We're trying to locate a 'Josephine Savage,'" he said.

"I'm Josephine Savage," she responded. A look of concern quickly spread about her face.

"Miss Savage, I'm Robert Kavanaugh, the District Attorney of Chatham County, Savannah Georgia. If possible, I'd like to ask you a few questions, please ma'am," Bobby requested.

JoJo immediately broke down in tears and wept uncontrollably. She went low on her knees and panted. Winston was forced to console and help his girlfriend gather herself once more, to engage in what the authorities wanted to question her about.

There was a brief moment between the time she broke down and got herself together. JoJo stood to her feet once more and waited in preparation for the cops to pronounce to her the words she long dreaded to her.

Winston spoke for her. "Officer, you may go ahead and ask her all you like, sir," he said.

"Very well. That, I shall do. Miss Savage, it was discovered that your lawfully wedded husband's name is Methuselah Savage, correct?" Bobby asked.

"That's correct, sir. But he and I are separated, as you may notice. And I'm now in the process of having a divorce performed from my husband," JoJo stated.

"—I'm sorry, Officers. Excuse me if you will," Winston butted in to say. "You still haven't let us know why you are here, or what these questions are pertaining to?"

Winston took Bobby by surprise in continuing to speak up for JoJo. Bobby was in the mindset that Josephine would simply begin to vehemently make pleas for mercy, while spewing her guts on all she had knowledge of. However, due to the proper training taught to JoJo by her father, to never speak at any time while in the presence of two men talking, she was able to avoid potential incrimination. This was especially so as it applied to the man of the house to visitors. And in the case of Winston being the man of the house and speaking for her, it made the situation easier to deal with.

On the other hand, Bobby held high expectations that he'd have the opportunity to lay eyes upon Mickey there at the residence, and be able to arrest him then and there, then extradite him back to Georgia. But, things didn't play out in that way. And so, Bobby had to work with what he had available, so as to get one step closer to nabbing who he wanted.

Bobby wanted to respond to what Winston stated to him. "Yes. The questions I'd like to ask Miss Savage is pertaining to her age at the time she married Methuselah Savage? I also have a few other questions I'd like to ask related to our potential suspect we have in Mr. Savage, aka 'Mickey Savage,'" Bobby said.

Winston looked at JoJo with a discerning demeanor expressed about his face. He then turned his head and looked back in Bobby's direction.

"May we step inside to discuss this, please?" Bobby asked. "This shouldn't take long, I wouldn't believe." Bobby spoke in a calm tone of voice so as to have the couple relax and not panic for any reason.

"Not a problem, Officers," responded Winston. "That sounds fair to me." He was eager himself to know more of the situation that was brewing. This would essentially provide Winston with more to use against Mickey to rid him from JoJo's life, faster than originally thought.

Everyone stepped inside. JoJo, Winston, and Bobby took a seat. The other men continued to stand. Bobby proceeded with the questioning.

"Miss Savage, could you please make me aware of your age at the time you got married?"

Reluctant at first, but then she went on with answering up to all asked.

"I was sixteen, sir. Soon to be seventeen."

"And are you aware that the man you married was ten years your senior? That he was a man involved in criminal activities? And that his troubles with the law were subject to affect all those he was in a relationship with?" Bobby posed strongly phrased questions.

"I'm aware that he was older than me. And everything we did was consensual. Nothing by force. But, as for the other stuff you mentioned, I know nothing about it. That was all his business. Not mine."

"Nothing by force, you say. But maybe something by fraud, possibly," Bobby stated. He had a sarcastic undertone to his voice and words.

"And how is that, sir?" Winston chimed in to ask.

"Well, for one, might I have you and Miss Savage to know in the great state of Georgia, the law prohibits a man of age to marry a girl who's not so. Underage marriage is illegal. And in this case, it was discovered that's what we have," Bobby revealed. He then pulled a document from the leather briefcase tote bag he carried.

Bobby held up the paper and continued to speak. "Now, according to this, it reads you were 'eighteen' years of age. However, you just confessed that you were only 'sixteen.' That's perjury. And in Georgia, a penalty of up to ten years in prison could be prescribed by law, if found guilty of this. A confession, Miss Lady, is the highest form of incrimination that there is. Do you wish to go to prison, ma'am?" Bobby muttered to spook her.

"No!" JoJo emphatically exclaimed. Her level of fear was elevated. She began to cry once more.

"Now you just hold on a minute there, sir! Do we need to contact a lawyer? Because Josephine has done nothing wrong," Winston stated in defense of his girlfriend.

"Nah, no lawyer necessary. And I didn't say she committed a crime, per se," Bobby stated, while looking Winston sternly in the eyes." I only stated what the document reads as and of what she said. Nothing further."

"Sir, I didn't have anything to do with the marriage document being written out and signed. Mickey had someone else do it all for us. I only agreed to it once it was done. That's it," JoJo said. "And again, I'm currently in the process of gaining a divorce from him. Once I got him to agree that this is best for us. That way, we can have this done without too much interference from a judge," JoJo stated.

"Do you have any information on how I may be able to locate him? Your husband, Methuselah Savage?"

"He lives in Philadelphia. I moved away a few years ago and haven't seen or heard from him throughout the time. You can find him there," JoJo responded.

"Oh, he lives in Philadelphia?" Bobby retorted.

"He lives in Philadelphia, sir. We are no longer together. I'm with this man now. And I'm also carrying his baby," JoJo let out in a snappy manner, having a look in Winston's direction at the same time.

"One last question for you, ma'am."

JoJo's heart began to beat rapidly behind Bobby's words. Her blood raced through her veins. She was on the verge of panicking.

Before Bobby was able to ask the last thing he had in mind, JoJo had thrown up. A portion of vomit spewed from her mouth onto the man's pants at the thigh area. They were seated across from one another. Bobby jolted backwards, then to his feet. She barfed once more, creating a bigger mess on the floor than was already there.

JoJo rushed to the bathroom at that point. Winston then interceded and brought the interview to an end.

"Gentlemen, I think my soon-to-be wife has had enough. So, if you don't have any authority to continue on with the line of questions you've asked of her, I'm afraid I'm gonna have to ask you to leave," stated Winston.

Bobby was already standing at this point. He had a few words to say prior to leaving.

"No, sir. I don't have any authority to proceed. However, I do have a line of serious questions I'd like to ask 'Mrs. Savage,' at some point soon when I return, about two of our finest policemen that are missing and may possibly be dead! I absolutely would like to know what she knows about this," Bobby said. "Oh, by the way, I never got your name, sir. Who am I speaking with?"

"My name is Winston. Winston Prather."

"Winston Prather … the boyfriend? Not Winston Prather, the husband? And you two have been together how long?" Bobby retorted. He attempted to belittle Winston and cause him to feel small and ashamed of his decision to be in a relationship with Josephine.

"Sir... have a nice day, will you?" Winston lastly stated. Bobby and the others then began to exit.

Bobby turned his body and spoke his last line of words. "I shall return with an arrest warrant. One for Methuselah Savage. And the other for his wife there," he said and pointed in the direction where JoJo last walked away. His words hit Winston below the belt. "The both of them will go down behind the issues related to those policemen. I promise you that!"

The door slammed behind the officers. Bobby was able to produce a smirk about his face in time for Winston to see. He felt that the interview worked in his favor. Winston no doubt had questions for his girlfriend, the one with the particular status as Bobby so sarcastically put it.

The pressure was now on for real, for JoJo to get the divorce from Mickey she so sought. Winston was at the point in their relationship where he demanded her obedience to his orders. Nothing less would do.

***

Johnny Mack eventually made up his mind to let Mickey in on the plot he'd conceived to forever eliminate the problems they wer experiencing with the law. He personally had grown sick and tired of living in fear and uncertainty. Not to mention the fact that his wife Natalie brought it to his attention that JoJo revealed to her, a Bobby Kavanaugh, showed up at her doorsteps and put her through a series of serious questions. JoJo told Natalie everything. This was because she knew Natalie would make known the same to Johnny Mack. And from Johnny Mack, word would then get to Mickey, the particular person she wanted to make aware without doing so directly. And so, just as bad as Johnny Mack was eager to take action, so was Mickey at this point.

Also, Johnny Mack heard from family down south in Georgia, that his cousin Otis, was arrested on murder charges, and showed a tendency that he would cooperate with the prosecuting attorney on making known the whereabouts of his brother, Mickey Savage.

So, I assume that's how that bastard Bobby was able to locate JoJo. Otis was the one who told him we moved north, Johnny Mack thought. *Mickey's muthafuckin' ass, seems to be laying it too safe. You can't hold your foot down on the head of a vicious rattlesnake and not expect it to bite you once you let up! You gotta crush the threat. And since Mickey can't do it, I will! My way!*

Along with the news about Bobby, Johnny Mack had a bit of tragic news to share with Mickey. His father had died, Johnny Mack's uncle. He was the uncle Johnny Mack looked up to most. Methuselah Savage, Sr.

The call was made to Mickey to make him aware. No other family members, other than Johnny Mack and Hound, had contact information to reach him. Therefore, the burden was left on Johnny Mack to deliver the bad news.

"Hello! Mickey here," he answered.

"Aye! Mickey, it's me, man. You situated in place for a moment?" Johnny Mack responded.

Mickey knew who the caller was. "Oh, hell! What now, Johnny Mack?"

"I may as well go ahead and spit it out, huh. Your daddy died this morning, family. My sister Alice called and let me know so I could let you know."

"Now I-be-damned! If it ain't one thing it's another, ain't it? Now I've got to deal with this. Life has a way to throw shit at you from every which way, don't it? I'll call you back later, Johnny Mack. Let me get in touch with the family down in Savannah and see what we got going on," Mickey stated.

"Okay. Take it easy, a'ight?"

The call between the two came to an end.

Mickey did his duty then and there and reached out to the family to provide his input on funeral arrangements. Once he was complete with that, he began to pack for the trip.

Although there wasn't a fugitive warrant to exist for his arrest, Mickey still felt the need to continue playing it safe while he was down in Bobby Kavanaugh's territory. Nonetheless, he and Johnny Mack had a trick up their sleeve on how they would deal with Bobby. The two Savage cousins were now all in on how they would deal with this vehement foe.

Chapter 23

One Week Later...
Boom!

The back door to Karen Marconi's home was knocked open by the force of an intruder's heavy foot. She was Angelo and Peter's sister. Also, the elderly lady was trusted with large amounts of cash and ingot bars of gold and silver. Her duty to the sibling Don Angelo was to operate as a safe-keep, and liaison with physical assets and towards businesspersons the family dealt with legitimately. Karen's address and contact information was inside the log-book Hound had possession of.

There were notes jotted down next to her name by Peter, detailing what all she held for them, each individual, and agendas she was due to perform. This was so regarding each individual listed. Peter had a terrible memory. And to aid and assist himself in keeping track, it was necessary to write things down as he had. And then, along came those Black Mafia goons who invaded his home with a robbery. And now, the plan was to go down the list and hit all other available locations where the mobsters stashed resources. It was Karen's turn to get it.

Hound wasn't in on this particular caper. He was away. Before he left, he'd put another of his Black Mafia brethren in charge, to go about and do the deeds of robberies from the log journal listings. There was a treasure trove of valuable information to be acted upon. And Russell Fitzgerald aka

"Big Stone," accompanied by three other Black Mafia soldiers, were the ones to do the acting.

The time was just past sunset when the caper took place. Karen lived at home alone. She'd been made a widow with the death of her husband from a heart attack, and their only born, a daughter, had long moved out.

Karen was seated in a recliner in the living room watching TV when the intruders forced their way inside.

"Oh my God! What's going on!" she yelled out behind the terrifying level of noise created when the door came open. She jolted from the chair and frantically looked around, trying to figure out what was going on in the back area of her home in south Philly.

Suddenly, a masked stocky figure raced towards her, grabbing ahold of and putting the old woman in the "full nelson" position. Another masked figure appeared. He was just as crude and rough with her as the first.

Whop!

He smacked her hard about the face.

Wham!

Then came a vicious backhand.

"Uh!"

And finally, a mean uppercut to the gut to complete the three-blow combination on the frail defenseless victim.

The hearty potato soup, string beans, and roll from earlier were spewed onto the floor. She puked her guts out behind the force of the blow. Karen was in pain and attempted to croak over, but wasn't able to from the position she was being held in. She could do nothing but cry.

The leader of the pact spoke at that point. "Now look, we can do this the hard way, or we can take the easy route. Have it how you like. Where is the money and the expensive jewelry?"

"I have no idea what you're talking about. And you're making a terrible mistake. If only you knew who my brothers are. They're gonna make you regret this," responded Karen.

Big Stone grinned from behind the ski mask. "Oh, really!"

Wham!

He backhanded her hard. Her face began to swell. Karen's body got weak. She went limp but wasn't allowed to fall.

"What about that! Will we regret that too?" Big Stone spat. "Let's try this again. We wanna know where the cash and the jewelry are. Give us what we want, and we'll leave you be, like you were when we came. And if you don't then, our response is simple. We kill you! Fuck your brothers! They must don't know who we are! We're Black Mafia! We are the ones who own the town and run the streets! And don't you forget that!"

"Damn you all! You despicable heathens! Go to hell!" Karen seemed to be more defiant now than she was to begin with.

"What!" retorted Stone.

He then clutched her around the throat with those big powerful hands of his. The six foot five frame and two hundred and fifty pounds of weight gave him the necessary strength to hold her in suspension off the floor as he choked the old lady.

"Who's the despicable heathen now, bitch! How about you go to hell, you fuckin' guinea slut!" Stone hissed through clench teeth.

She'd really pissed him off. Seriously.

Karen kicked and slapped at Stone until she could no more in her futile attempts to fight him to turn her loose. And then, a stream of urine trailed from under her gown, down her leg and dripped continuously to the floor, followed by her body going completely limp. Life had literally been choked from her.

Big Stone unclutched his grip. Karn's frail thin body dropped hard to the floor, creating an unforgettable thud. In this, something about the floor was detected. There was a hollow sound to it. Nothing solid.

"Y'all catch that too, fam?" he asked of the other two. They both nodded, yes, they had.

Stone began to stomp his foot in the area where the body and recliner seat was situated. He pushed the chair out the way and had one of the others drag Karen out the way by the arm. He stomped again in the exact spot where the chair was.

"I think we might got something down there," said Stone.

"I think we do too," responded the third man.

They all pulled the carpet from the wall halfway across the floor.

"Bingo!" Stone let out at the sight of the draw-flap panel. It was a compartment. There was a pull handle to it.

Stone reached down and opened. There in the compartment sat square blocks of cash tightly wrapped in plastic and tape.

"Now this is what the fuck I'm talkin' about! Everything we came here for!" Stone exclaimed in excitement. They began to pull everything from the compartment. The robbery turned out to be worth it.

In addition to the three million in cash they found, they got away with one million in gold and silver mini-ingot bars. The information from the address book proved to be correct. It was now on to the next one.

***

Mickey, Johnny Mack, Hound, and a good friend of theirs, were down in Georgia, in advance of the date of the funeral for Mickey's father. The Savage family was a large one, with many appearing from far and wide to pay their respects.

Aside from the obvious reason they were there in the Peach State, there was a scheme that had been hatched in mind, to potentially perpetuate against Bobby. The plan was to have this carried out prior to the actual day of Mickey's father's homegoing service.

Mickey strongly felt that in order for him to have a peaceful day to lay his father to rest, without any disturbance from anyone in law enforcement, the main man Bobby, had to be completely out the way. He knew Bobby had knowledge of his father's passing, due to the brother Otis being locked up and cooperating. And without a doubt, Bobby also knew that the best opportunity he had to nail Mickey would be to capture him at the funeral. Bobby anticipated the moment.

On the flip side of things, Mickey was aware of where Bobby lived. He'd been to his home before. And although Bobby and the wife were going through a divorce process, Bobby still lived on the premises of the estate, though not inside the mini mansion. He stayed in the guest house out back. Bobby utilized the space as a "man-cave." Mickey was aware of this as well. He recalled a time when Bobby mentioned something to the effect of taking residence in the guest house specifically, at any time he and the wife were to have issues in their marriage. The divorce process was no different.

***

The day was a Friday evening, one day prior to the actual funeral date. The sun was beginning to set. The rural area where Bobby lived was turning silent as it always does around the time each day. Bobby had had a long day at work in the office. He'd been busy putting together an arrest unit of officers who were to be at his command, for the take down of Mickey and potentially Johnny Mack come the next day, as they attended the funeral. Otis had informed that Mickey would surely risk it all to be there. So would Johnny Mack.

Bobby honestly didn't give a damn. He had the gall and audacity with his decision making, to bum-rush the man's father's funeral, so to slap cuffs on him, in the presence of family who would be looking on. However, Johnny Mack, not Mickey, made proper preparation in advance to put forth the strongest fight against Bobby, and to see to it that no interference happened. Johnny Mack was determined to see to it that his plot would work. Mickey had no idea how thorough and detailed his cousin's scheme was.

Bobby's home sat on an acreage of pine trees. There were also other bushy brushes. The estate was an enclave within the woods. The driveway was a long "S" shape from the highway to the front door. Maybe a half mile in length.

Bobby had a deer stand on the property not far in distance from the house. Wild game of deer, turkey, quail, coon, and on occasion, feral hogs roamed through. He hunted as sport when his time permitted. But, since being elected as the official D.A., he hadn't been able to do what he enjoyed for recreation often. When on vacation, he was in the habit.

Bobby got out of his car and made steps towards the front door of the guest house. He put the key into the deadbolt lock and was about to turn it to open. Suddenly …

Ptui!

A lethal round spit from the barrel of the silencer muffled rifle of the assassin. The high caliber bullet penetrated the upper left area of Bobby's back, through the heart, out his chest, and through the front door of the guest house. He dropped to his knees and then collapsed onto the cement porch. The man known as Bobby Francis Kavanaugh, was dead in a matter of seconds.

Frank took the shot from Bobby's deer stand that was situated roughly seventy-five yards from the house. This turned out to be a sure shot for the military trained sniper. He was just the type of hitter Johnny Mack needed him to be.

Once the job was completed, Frank hurried and climbed down from the fifty-foot stand, raced through the woods to the opposite side, got into the getaway car, and hauled ass back north en route to Philly. I-95 was a straight shot.

Mickey, Johnny Mack, and Hound, would all hear about the well-done job on the news or read about it in the papers.

By that time, the assassin would be long gone and known nothing about. The Savage boys would now have the leeway to gain a peace of mind and experience relief. The legal threat and vehement enemy had finally been put down. For good. Bobby was no more.

Chapter 24

One Day Later...

Mickey and the Savage family saw to it that his father was properly laid to rest. The service lasted from 11:00 a.m. to 1:00 p.m. Around the two o'clock hour, the breaking news continuation from earlier reported that the once highly respected and pronounced prosecutor, Robert F. Kavanaugh took an assassin's bullet to the back. The authorities had no idea where to begin with the investigation of the killing. They would never make themselves come to believe that a Negro shooter was cut out to pull off such a high-profile slaying, and the truth would never be spoken upon.

Mickey and Johnny Mack simply look on at the TV screen and at one another displaying pleasant smiles. They'd pulled it off. Johnny Mack had at least. The hit on Bobby was as big to them as was the hit on the 35th President of the United States to the mafia. According to how media talking heads speculated.

The boys high-five one another and gave praise to the brave man Frank, for pulling the trigger, and to a future that was to be now worry free.

Mickey got on the phone to call Miss Peaches. He wanted her to know that she could now breathe easy, and to be prepared to cash in on the insurance policy over Bobby's death.

"Miss Peaches here," she answered.

"Peaches! It's me, Mickey," he responded.

"I'm aware." She caught the voice. "Why you sound so happy?"

She was under the impression that he was to be a sad man behind the death of his father.

"I got good reason to be happy. You're about to be too, once I tell you what I'm about to say."

"And what is it you got to tell me, Mickey Savage?"

"Bobby! The son of a bitch is dead!" he revealed to her.

"You bullshittin' me, ain't you!" Peaches responded.

"Nope! I'm not. I'm looking at the news now. Turns out, the bastard took a bullet to the back. He had just gotten home from work."

"Oh my! I wonder who he pissed off? He was always busy scheming to do somebody wrong. I guess he won't be able to no more," said Peaches. She apparently expressed a breath of relief and delight in the same thread of speech.

"That muthafucka' did something dirty! But it was to the wrong person. He got what he deserved. And I don't feel sorry for his ass either! That bastard tried to kill me, you, and your baby. He didn't succeed though. Justice has its way of looking out for the innocent," Mickey stated.

"So, I guess that insurance policy thing was a good idea after all, huh," Miss Peaches uttered. The thought was that she could cash in sooner rather than later.

"Oh, yeah! Indeed it was... indeed it was, Miss Peaches. And all the shit we went through with Bobby is about to pay off, baby girl. You and Sparkle might wanna pack up and head down here in the next couple of days. That way, you can go to the places you need to and make your claims."

"Okay, Mickey. I'll see you when we get down there."

"Okay, babe. Y'all travel safely, you hear," Mickey lastly said.

The call ended.

Mickey stepped back into the room where Johnny Mack and Hound sat. He and Johnny Mack continued to look at one another and smile. Hound knew himself about the plot to have Frank pull the trigger. Even before Mickey knew a thing. Neither Johnny Mack or Hound made Mickey know exactly of the details of how things were to go. Frank was told to keep things away from Mickey as well until the time was right. And at that particular moment, the time was right. They finally revealed everything to Mickey.

The pressure Bobby applied was relieved. His assassin made it all possible. The threat behind killing those two cops was eliminated. Mickey could rest easy at night with no more anxiety. He was good to go.

Chapter 25

Several Months Later...

JoJo gave birth to a baby boy. She and Winston named him after Winston at his christening. Winston couldn't have been a happier man than he was that day, the moment his son came into the world. One part of what he wanted with JoJo was complete with two more to go. Have her legitimately gain a divorce from Mickey, and then, the two of them get married. Also, Winston had the idea in mind to send her oldest three sons, Josh, Ishmael, and Isaac, to live with their father. The girls too, if he could get JoJo to agree to the terms. Winston wanted only to have his family there with him in the house and not have the responsibility of taking care of another man's kids, let alone five of them. This was something he was initially willing to do, up to the point of now having a child of his own.

JoJo and Winston's son was now six months in age. To the other kids, their mother seemed to look after and care for him in a far better way than she did them. JoJo failed to take notice of the ill-feelings she caused and wasn't able to correct the situation before those ill-feelings took root and created a negative effect. Also, Mickey's kids wanted to see him, so they could let him know what was going on at their house in New Hampshire. They hadn't seen him since the year prior, when they were on summer break.

Not long after the day JoJo gave birth to the last child, she and Winston began a follow-up on the issue Bobby came to her about. JoJo figured that by giving a confession on the action that Mickey took to make her his wife, it could be utilized to help her out of the legal bind she was in with him. Something she wanted nothing to do with any longer. Repeated attempts were made to contact the District Attorney.

When the call was made by JoJo to his office, she learned that the prosecutor was no more. He was deceased. And that a new official replaced him. No knowledge of the situation was known by them. Therefore, JoJo's only other option at that point, was to travel to Philly on her own accord, and have a conversation with her husband and do all necessary to persuade Mickey to sign off on the divorce papers, and free her of him and his name. The only thing left to question was, would he be willing to do so?

JoJo hit the highway on the trip to Philly. Mickey had no heads up that she was on the way. It would be a surprise visit. JoJo didn't want him to know, as her suddenness, would be intended to have a certain element to it. That way, she might be able to convince him that maybe a divorce would be the right way to re-establish the peace between them.

JoJo knew Mickey very well. She was aware of how calculated and routine he was with time scheduling and how he went about his day. It was the weekend. A Saturday. The time was near 11:00 a.m. There was only one place she knew her husband would be situated at that hour. Somewhere he religiously visited every week whether rain, sleet, snow, or a hailstorm. Mickey would be at this spot, no matter what.

JoJo parked her car in the lot next to the establishment she intended to enter. She got out, checked herself in the handheld mirror she carried, put it back in her purse, and made steps to the front door of the building. Upon entering, the bell above the door tingled. All the men situated inside, along with a few women, turned their heads in the direction where JoJo now stood, roving her head in search for a familiar face. She located him. The two locked eyes.

Mickey was seated in the barber's chair and in the process of having his head and face shaved clean with a straight razor when JoJo appeared. She simply smiled at him and took a seat herself.

Look at Mickey. Ain't changed a bit in being so routine. I knew I'd find him here. It's one of his pet-peeves, JoJo thought.

"Hey, Mickey!" she greeted. "Go on ahead and get yourself groomed. I'll sit patiently right here for you, ok, babe? I have plenty of time. I came to talk with you anyway. I'm by myself," she added.

Once Mickey was done at the barber shop, he and JoJo followed one another to the main house where they once lived together. He still stayed there from time-to-time. At least a day or two out of the week.

"This place been empty as hell since you took the kids and left me for dead all by my lonely," Mickey said. "It's good to see you again though. It's been so long. I almost forgot what you looked like," he let out with a slight laugh.

JoJo smiled delightfully. "Mmm-hmm! Don't give me that lonely mess, Mickey Savage. I'm sure that your girl Peaches, or the other one, Sparkle, kept you with more than enough company between the time," JoJo responded in a nonchalant manner.

"How you know about Sparkle, JoJo?"

"My girls told me all about her. They say she showed them a really good time. They like her."

"Oh!" he let out with a smile. "I forgot about that."

They took a seat in the living room across from one another.

"I don't see any evidence of no one living here other than you," JoJo remarked.

"Only me here. My other house is where me and Sparkle stay. But I'm curious to know what you got on your mind to talk about, that caused you to drive from New Hampshire to see me all by yourself? And as long as you been gone, you finally decided to do the right thing and face me, so we can have a conversation over the problems we have."

"No! Over the problems that we had, Mickey. At the time, But apparently, that's no more. I heard Bobby died. So, our secret about what really happened that night is still just that, a secret. I assume we ain't got to worry no more. I hope not."

"And I see you didn't hate me to the point where you would rat me out to Bobby and have me locked up when he paid you a visit. I thank you for that," Mickey stated.

"I didn't rat you out, because I finally came to realize that what you'd done, was the right thing to have done. You protected your pregnant wife and our home. That's what any real man is supposed to do."

"So why the hell you up and leave me like that then? Why didn't you stay by my side like you were supposed to?" Mickey's questions had a depth of seriousness to them.

"Because I was scared, Mickey. That's why. And on top of that, you were too busy out there in those streets generating more problems to bring home to your family. It became too much for me. And I knew that no matter what, you weren't gonna stop being who you are and doing what you do. You're just as reluctant to change as you wanna be, Mickey Savage. You're so unwilling to change and continue on about life, doing the right thing. And I'm sure now, you still haven't. I don't even have to ask."

Chapter 26

Mickey lowered his head in a shameful manner behind JoJo's words. This was an admission of guilt on his behalf.

JoJo continued to speak. "But look. All of that is neither here nor there at this point. And just so you'll know, I still love you. I just don't like you anymore. And I don't want nothing to do with you and the marriage. That's why I'm here to talk with you. Amongst other things," she stated.

"You don't even sound the same no more, JoJo. You been around those white people too long, I see," Mickey responded.

"That's true. You're right about that. I have been around those white people too long. And had I not, I probably wouldn't be the woman I am to this day. Or, in the position I now am to succeed. Your kids benefit in a major way from being around those white people more than you may ever know. But I'm not looking to have that type of conversion with you, Mickey. Because I honestly do want you to be a part of your kids' lives. I will never do anything to prevent that."

"And what else do you want from me, JoJo? Let's go ahead and put it all out there, shall we?" Mickey said to urge her to get to the exact reason why she was there.

"That will be my pleasure, Mickey, to let you know what I want from you. Actually, it's two things. Hopefully we can come to a peaceful agreement about them both."

"—Get on with it, JoJo, will you please? Stop holding it back," he demanded.

"I want a divorce from you. The marriage license was forged anyway, so we've been illegitimately married all this time to begin with. And once I'm out of wedlock with you, I could then move on with my life and get married to someone else," JoJo expressed her desires to be freed from him. "And, once that's done, I want you to take full responsibility as a man and raise your three boys we have. Here in Philly with you, that is. Under your roof. I can handle the girls. Can we agree to that?" JoJo stated as she sat back in the chair, crossed her legs casually, and awaited Mickey to reply to all she'd said.

He smiled, got up from his seat, and walked over to take a position next to JoJo on the couch.

"Mickey, don't start with that, ok? We are not even like that anymore. I've moved on from you. I'm with somebody else now," she said and stretched out her arm to keep him at a distance.

He sat back in the seat next to JoJo and began to behave himself once more. These sexual impulses he felt for JoJo could be a bit uncontrollable at times for Mickey. This was the first and only time she'd turned him away sexually.

"I tell you what, Josephine. This is what I'm willing to do. I'll sign any divorce papers you need me to sign. But, only under one condition." He laid out an ultimatum.

"And what might that one condition be? That I have sex with you?"

Mickey smiled at her response.

"I strongly feel that we have to end things on a peaceful note, if we are to indeed end it. And besides, you still are my wife, you know. You don't belong to that white boy Winston just yet. You still got my last name … Savage! How sweet the sound," Mickey boasted.

"Mickey! We are ending things on a peaceful note. That's why I'm here. And, you know how faithful and committed I am to somebody that I'm in a relationship with. So, let's be mindful that not one time did I cheat on you. Not once. And as bad as my body wouldn't mind feeling your strong manhood inside of me, I can't put myself up to doing Winston wrong. No matter how much better you are sexually than him. That white boy, as you put it, accepted me and all five of my damn kids, and provided us a life that's worthy of a fairytale story. Now how can I disrespect a man who does that?" JoJo stated emphatically.

"And that's why you gave him a baby, huh?" Mickey retorted.

"The reason why I gave him a baby was because he proved to be deserving of one. A son. We named him after his father. He's a junior."

"So, I guess signing any divorce papers at this point is off the table then, huh? No more negotiations I guess?"

JoJo shook her head in pity at Mickey. "Methuselah Savage. You ought to be ashamed of yourself. You don't want to give me an honorable divorce, because I won't give into you sexually. Why, Mickey? Why must it be this way? Is sex that important to you? I'm sure you got Sparkle, Miss Peaches, and Lord knows whoever else, to please you in that way."

"Yeah, but ain't but one Josephine Savage. And you the only one to make me feel the way only you know how."

She shook her head yet again at his remark. "Like I said, Mickey. As bad as my body wants to, I can't. But, we can go out to dinner and do romantic things together, if you're cool with only that? I'm here in Philly until Monday. Now, if we can stop talking about us having sex for a moment and focus on the subject about our boys, that'll be better. They're your responsibility to raise, Mickey. Your sons. You should be willing to do that."

"And I am willing to do that, JoJo. I just need you to give me a little time to prepare myself. This was a sudden thing on me," he declared.

"How much time you need?"

"I can't say right off. I'll let you know. But you gotta be sure to keep in touch. I ain't seen or heard from you in a few years. You just up and hauled ass on me. And took half my money while you was at it. But I'm cool with that. My kids was taken care of with it, I'm sure."

"Absolutely they were. But, I need to know something sooner rather than later, Mickey."

"Winston tryna clean house already I see. Goddamn! But that's understandable. Every lion in the jungle does kill off all the cubs of the other lion, to make his own with the lioness. And now, since you gave him a son, he wants me to take mine in, so he could make more of his own."

"And how you come to that conclusion?" JoJo asked.

"As much as you adore them boys, I know this ain't your call. Now, is it? Tell me the truth. I can see straight through that."

JoJo took a long pause before offering to answer his question. She hated the fact whenever Mickey called her out on her shit. It used to be her always doing so unto him. But the shoe was on the other foot now. And he had the lead on the conclusion to things.

"No, Mickey. It's not my call, alright. Winston wanted this. And I couldn't tell him not to want this for what he's trying to establish. Besides, it's better for the boys, I believe," JoJo responded honestly.

"I assume y'all two gonna be busy tryna make more babies in the near future, huh?"

"We may. But that's me and Winston's business, Mickey. Not you and I."

"Understood. But this is what I'm willing to compromise with you on. Until I'm properly situated to take on the boys full-time, I can keep them in summers, spring breaks, and other breaks they may have, if they wanna come and stay with me during those times. But during summer and spring breaks, they don't have a choice. We make that decision for them. You okay with that?" Mickey asked of her.

"I can't make a complaint about it. That's a start. Considering the fact of who you are, and all the things you got going on. But, you could do better, Mickey. You just don't want to," JoJo responded.

"And I will do better. Just allow me the time I need to make the situation right. And once that happens, I'll be more than willing to take on my boys full-time. Ok?" Mickey stated. He seemed to be on the verge of getting frustrated. More so from the sexual impulses and being denied by JoJo than anything else.

JoJo looked on at him and shook her head once more. She knew what type of withdrawals he was experiencing. Sex was utilized by her as a tool against him before. But not in a harsh way.

"I wanna know something, JoJo."

"Ask me all you like, Mickey. That's why I'm here. To talk with you and we get everything out the way we got on our chest."

"What I wanted to ask was, why did you just leave on me without so much as being willing to sit down and talk with me about it?"

"Mickey … I don't believe you'll ever know or understand how much you ruined my life. All my hopes and dreams eventually turned into only a fantasy and a nightmare," JoJo spoke candidly to him. She didn't want to hold back any longer with what she'd been holding onto since 1958.

"Damn, JoJo! Why you say it like that?"

"Because Mickey … that's the truth on how I feel. I had just graduated high school when we met. I was supposed to have been on my way to one of the top HBCU's in the country—Howard in DC perhaps—to be a doctor … a dentist … a lawyer … or some type of professional. And then, along came ol' sly Mickey, waggling his slick tongue, using his deceptive mind, and doing everything possible to get me and take my virginity away, he and that poisonous black snake he has between his legs. You got me pregnant five times, Mickey Savage. And not once did you take out the time to think to yourself that you need to go legit and stay that way. At least for the sake of your seven children. Not just for yourself. That's what a responsible man would do. This is the main reason why I love and respect my 'country-ass' daddy the way I do. Because he's a man! A real man! We may not have had much. But he worked like hell to take care of his wife and five kids. And he took nothing for granted. He didn't ever risk being taken away from his family. Daddy valued and appreciated his freedom. Something I would like to see you begin doing."

JoJo gave a long monologue on exactly how she felt.

"Wow! That was a lot, JoJo. a lot. Such strong words coming from you," Mickey responded.

"That's eight years' worth of shit I've been holding onto. It was time for it all to come out. But look. I'm tired from the long drive. I need a bath, some rest, and a good meal when I wake up."

"Where you plan on staying?"

JoJo threw her hands high, shrugged her shoulders, pursed her lips, and cocked her head to one side to concede!

"Where else am I gonna stay, Mickey Savage? I'm home, ain't I? If only but for a few days," she let out.

Mickey smiled happily as ever. He made his way out to her car to get her bags of luggage. The two had so much to talk about and catch up on. However, as "friends" this time around. Not so much as the loving married couple that they once were. What such turn of events.

Chapter 27

Later in the evening, Mickey took JoJo out to dinner and a movie. When they returned to the house, he tried with all he had to have some of her sexually. JoJo didn't go for anything strange because that's what he was to her now. However, they came to the agreement to get along for the sake of getting along, so as to at least keep the love and the peace in place. Part of the deal was to be no sex and no passionate kissing. Mickey accepted. This made it possible for JoJo to become comfortable with being around him while in the nude. But at the same time, JoJo knew she had to get the monkey off his back in some kind of way, to keep him calm and not be overtaken by his sexual desires. So, what she allowed was for him to get naked himself, along with her, straddle atop her hindlegs while she lay across the bed eating fruit from a bowl and watching TV, and masturbate his manhood, releasing his load onto her buttocks.

Once complete, she sensuously caressed his love potion all about her rear end with the palms of her hands. They both took turns in the bathroom washing up. Moving forward, she didn't want to do anything to sexually arouse him anymore. Mickey had no choice but to respect the boundary lines JoJo had set in place, to keep things cordial and copacetic between them. They went so far as to sleep in separate rooms of the house. Friendship and a shared parenthood was all JoJo honestly wanted. Nothing more. Mickey finally came to realize the understanding JoJo wanted to establish with him. She was successful at communicating this well to him, in words and through action.

The coming summer, Mickey was intent on keeping his boys. His vow was that in due time, he'd take them on full-time. Nonetheless, he still refused to peacefully go his own separate way. He didn't sign the divorce papers she presented to him. He couldn't. Pride, ego, and stubbornness prevented. Also, his love and sexual desire for her was too intense to simply allow her to walk away and no longer carry his last name. He really hated the idea that she was looking to escape him and go marry someone else. A fucking white boy at that! He vented. There was no way Mickey Savage could come to grips with reality in knowing he'd lost his wife to a white boy! He made this fact well known to JoJo why he couldn't push himself to do so. And to prevent an argument, JoJo decided to put divorce talks off for a later date and time. A suitable thing to do in Mickey's eyes and mind.

Josephine's visit to Philly and meeting up with her lawfully wedded husband went well, for the most part. But, once back at home in New Hampshire, her explanation to Winston was subject to cause him to think and become indifferent in a way. He might turn livid behind Mickey's refusal. Maybe a meeting between them would be necessary. Nothing was off the table.

Part Two

Chapter 28

A Few Years Later...

Things began to pay off for Miss Peaches following Bobby's death. It took her just over a year to show and prove to the court, to the bank Bobby had business with, and to the insurance company that she took out a policy with, that Bobby fathered a son by her. But once this process was complete, the benefits of it all began to take root and come into fruition.

To Miss Peaches' surprise, Bobby had long ago set up a trust account for all of the kids he had and the future ones that were to come. The funds were to be retrieved upon his death. His will indicated the same. These accounts were set up prior to his second child being born. The Kavanaugh clan was a rich and wealthy delegated family of people in the coastal empire of Georgia. They had corporations, businesses and properties, both commercial and residential, and the proceeds from those entities funded the trust accounts Bobby opened for his kids.

There was six million dollars the kids were to split. He had two daughters with his wife, and also a son by Peaches. There were college tuition funds to be inherited upon completion of high school. However, Bobby was sure to include one stipulation, that all his kids must pursue a career in the legal profession to become attorneys. Prosecuting lawyers was Bobby's wish. His desire was to establish a lineage of attorneys who would turn out to be just like him, he wouldn't have it any other way.

Therefore, Miss Peaches had to make a decision then and there under penalty of perjury, to have her son grow up and become an attorney, so as to get the money. She was made aware of this by the lawyer who represented her. The court was compelled by the preponderance of the evidence and a conclusion of law, to rule in favor of Peaches against that of the Kavanaughs.

Roughly a month after having the two million transferred to her bank account, along with the seven-million-dollar settlement claim from the insurance policy, Peaches was the one to keep it all the way real with Mickey and gave him half the money she had. The two then agreed to go on about life as platonic friends like they'd been for many years. And at the same time, she wanted to move along on her own accord and be no longer under the dictation of Mickey. Peaches wanted to travel and be free spirited while spending quality time with her son. There was a desire to do what she pleased.

Miss Peaches was intent on buying a home in three different locations, one in Savannah for sure, one in the Bahamas, and one in Philly. She also wanted to own a business and continuously turn a buck so as not to go broke. Good use had to be made of the money.

And so, a life for Miss Peaches opposite Mickey leading the way and providing for her, had begun. The two would be sure to keep contact and visit one another from time-to-time. This was part of the agreement.

Likewise, the bond between Peaches and Sparkle remained intact. Although not sharing as much time together as before, the two had a love and appreciation for one another the world over. However, the fun they used to have while out and about in the streets, shopping, or during girl time talking, would be missed most. The two moved on about life re-establishing different goals and to-do agendas. Peaches now had a son to raise. One to become an attorney, then possibly a judge. And Sparkle, she had no kids but badly wanted one. She and Mickey was busy trying to make this a reality.

***

Mickey was sure to keep to his word and took responsibility over his boys during school breaks. Throughout the summers over the few years since JoJo went to Philly to have the conversation with Mickey, his three sons lived with him. The girls were away as well. In Georgia at times, or with their aunt Sasha. JoJo and Winston had only their son to deal with during these times. This was the intended household structure Winston wanted and had in mind. Slowly he insinuated the thought to JoJo. He wanted Mickey to take on all of his children full-time as a real man would, since he didn't want to divorce JoJo.

This created a problem between Winston and JoJo. One she needed to resolve the best way she could, so as to not have Winston dump her and move on to someone else. But little did she know, her boys by Mickey, complicated things even more by telling their father how much better their mother tended to treat and care after "Little Winston" over them. Whether JoJo did this unconsciously or not, the damage was done.

Atop the boys feeling less than, the girls, particularly Mary, were continuously preyed more aggressively now, as she was older, and began to spread more through her initial stages of puberty. This pursuit of the little girl was at school with the young boys and at home with Winston. He was now at the point of fully molesting Mary by penetrating her private areas. He would also perform cunnilingus acts on her. Winston had gotten out of hand and was wrong every which way.

To keep Mary silent about what he was doing to her, he'd treat her to extra snacks throughout the week after school, such as candy, cookies, and ice cream. And at times, he'd slip a couple of quarters into her panties to surprise her with. His advantage with the snacks was so because JoJo denied them treats Monday through Thursday. On the days Winston was looking to perpetuate his acts upon her, he'd call Mary into the pantry, do his evil, then have her eat the goodies there out of sight of the other kids. Some days, he'd bring special treats home for her to further manipulate the girl. Expensive kinds she'd only seen on TV, or heard her schoolteacher talk to other teachers about.

His intention was to make her feel good about what they were doing and cause her to desire it more. She was forced to keep quiet about all that had taken place. Not to mention the fact that JoJo visually shows profound love and affection to her biracial child more so than the others. This brought out hurt and other ill-feelings from Mary, in addition to the anger and frustration her mother often expressed about their father, and how "less of a man" he was in comparison to Winston or their grandfather down in Georgia. Someone Mary absolutely knew nothing about.

Winston was masterful in his diabolical machinations and designs. He'd made it to where Mary became ok with the things going on between the two. She said not a word. The perversion continued.

***

Throughout the time following the failed hit on his life, Don Angelo Marconi was made aware of who it was that tried to take him out. He and his goons were successful in tracking down the two shooters who remained at large and put an end to them. They'd gotten whacked in the worst way, stuffed in oil barrels, had concrete mix poured atop their bodies, then dumped in the Schuylkill River. Before the men were killed, they spewed their guts on all they knew of the plot. As suspected, Dolan Estafan was behind it all. He wouldn't be reached, due to running to the feds out of fear of his own life and that of his family being endangered.

Dolan ratted about all he had first-hand knowledge of, regarding crimes that had been committed on the orders of Don Angelo. That of murder is to be included. Even the ones he committed himself for his boss. In order to receive witness protection, Dolan had to tell everything he'd done throughout his tenure in the mob. Also, when the time was to be at hand, he would be obligated to testify against Don Angelo.

During this time, the government was in its early stages of what would become known as the Racketeer Influenced and Corrupt Organizations Act, or the "RICO" Act for short. And when they were to come for the seemingly untouchable Don Angelo, they had intentions to hit him hard. An investigation of intense magnitude had begun of the Marconi crime family.

Don Angelo often retreated to a cabin house he owned in the Pocono region of Pennsylvania during these times. He would leave his brother Peter and son Raphael over the operations. Mainly the narcotic business they thrived in. However, when Don Angelo was contacted by Mickey, and made aware he had two point five million to spend on product, he desired to personally fulfill the order. That way, he could also have a conversation with Mickey and be enlightened of his progress in the streets. This would be by far the largest purchase Mickey had ever put in for, and Don Angelo wanted to offer a smile, shake his hand, and wish him well with the business. The bond between the two was solid.

***

Hound was finally able to convince Mickey and Johnny Mack to become Black Mafia. They were to serve as the brains and architects behind the administrative body that was deformed. A body of nine figureheads. Something similar to the U.S. Supreme Court. It was those three, Frank, Big Stone, and four others to make up the council. And so, it was the Black Mafia Family originating in Philly, alongside the Italian Mafia who supplied the product.

Basically, BMF had a chokehold on north Philly, west, southwest, and certain parts of south Philly. The group was rapidly growing by the day. Mickey had a natural way of displaying persuasion and influential leadership. Everyone began to perceive he was the leader, because of his charming ways and diplomatic skills. The council of nine called all the shots, maintained rule, and decreed orders. Mickey was at the helm. The streets and hoods in the black community viewed him as a "Don," a "Godfather," and a "Gangsta-Elite." They looked up to him. Much the same as a head of the various Italian mob units looked up to their own. Mickey had power outside of official power. His position became a very important one, and he embraced everything that came along with it.

Mickey bought a building in north Philly. It was renovated and converted into a diner. This served as an office. The location was at Germantown and Erie Avenues.

Chapter 29

Lacy Smith's family put out a missing person's report over his sudden disappearance at the time. They had no knowledge of what actually happened to him or where to begin a search of their own. The Philly PD was contacted by the federal government regarding a confidential informant, Dolan, reporting to them that he knew something about what went on with a black drug dealer who was on their missing list.

The informant stated that the Italian mafia crime family headed by Angelo Marconi, had the guy executed over a home invasion where drugs were taken. Even with the informant far away in the state of Utah and under a different identity, he still provided valuable information regarding Lacy's situation, to help build the case the feds were structuring, so as to nab Don Angelo and put him away for a long time to come. They needed as much as could be mustered up to make their case stronger.

The informant gave them the name of a female who was mentioned while he was in the ranks of the mob. She formerly danced at a bar owned by a mafia capo of Marconi. A guy by the name of Joey.

Philly police investigators maintained records of the last places Lacy visited prior to going missing. This practice was part of the case to find out what potentially happened with him. There was one particular establishment to stand out. This was a luxury hotel in downtown Philly. Lacy and a female named Victoria Tarquinii, reserved a suite together at the time. Both names appeared on the registration.

At the point of Victoria no longer being needed by Joey after trapping Lacy, she took off and moved away to Allentown, Pennsylvania. Philly homicide issued a warrant for her from the statements made by the federal informant. Victoria was involved in an auto accident there in Allentown. She'd rear-ended someone while under the influence of alcohol. She was charged and booked. The warrant from Philly surfaced. She wasn't aware that she'd been a fugitive. The young lady was transported to Philly, drilled intensely with questions and held without bond. Throughout the process, she broke and told all she'd done, all she knew, and who the person was to put her up to it.

In addition to the cops having Victoria and a confession, they also had a recording. Somehow, the federal informant managed to steal the tape from Don Angelo. Victoria's voice was clearly heard. This corroborated her confession. The police knew then that Lacy had been murdered. He was no longer of the status of "missing person."

Because of the things mentioned on the tape between Lacy and Victoria, the feds and Philly police were now in the know of many things they once knew nothing about. They knew that a "Black Mafia" existed in the streets, they knew that the Maroni crime family was responsible for Lacy's killing. They knew that a rival mafia member named "Nimble Neil," set up the home invasion of Peter Marconi and because of such, Neil was possibly tracked down and killed as well. They knew that a capo named Joey Logano, was an enforcer and likely the one who killed Lacy, Neil, and possibly more, under the orders of Angelo Marconi. Also, the authorities now knew that the Marconi family were the prime suppliers of heroin in Philly.

There were overwhelming elements of probable cause established. The feds secured an arrest warrant through the indictment process. They intended to take down Angelo

Marconi, his brother Peter, Joey Logano, and five other mafioso of Marconi.

The elite of the French Connection had dirty agents on payroll there in Philly. They knew of Don Angelo's impending arrest and shut down all business with the family. Nothing more was to be done with them. At least not at the time. They were no longer good for business.

***

Mickey and his people had six million worth of supply. That was the three million he, Johnny Mack, and Hound bought together, and the three million Don Angelo gave on consignment. The transaction occurred pre-indictment.

On the morning of the raid and execution of the indictment, Mickey and Hound lounged at the diner Mickey owned. They looked on at the news as it was being reported.

"Well, I-be-damned!" exclaimed Mickey. "Ain't this a bitch!"

"Goddamn sho' is!" Hound responded. "Looks like we gotta find another supplier now, don't we!"

"Hell, yeah! Or leave this shit alone all together and find something better to do," Mickey stated. He was being honest about his thoughts through his words.

Johnny Mack was in the restroom. He'd returned to the presence of the other two and caught notice of what was on display in the media.

"You see that, Johnny Mack?" asked Hound.

"What the fuck! Hell yeah, I do! Those sons of a bitches arresting Don Angelo and his people, ain't they!" Johnny Mack responded.

"Sho' is," chimed Mickey. "And like I was just saying to Hound, maybe that's a sign to leave this shit alone altogether and find something better to do with our lives."

"Huh!" expressed Johnny Mack. "I ain't so sure about all that, Mickey. I don't think I'll ever let go of the game. Only evolve in it to become a better businessman at what I do while in the game. That be it," Johnny Mack countered.

His thing was, he strongly felt he hadn't made enough money yet to retire from the dope game, also he didn't know how much money his two cousins had put away. All Johnny Mack knew was how much drugs they had left on hand. He'd put up one million of his own money towards it. Mickey never mentioned the kilos he was provided on consignment. Only gave Johnny Mack and Hound what they'd paid for.

Mickey continued with what he had on his mind.

"I'm thinking about the future of my kids, you two. I been a poor father. And I hate to think of myself as anything that low. But it's the truth. I abandoned my duties as a man. And I'm a coward for that," Mickey stated. The conversation he and JoJo had that time was eating at him.

Hound felt the need to respond to those words. "Nigga, please! Don't have no goddamn pity-party with yourself at our expense! We done came too far for that shit, Mickey."

"Damn sho' have!" inserted Johnny Mack.

Mickey now turned his head to address him specifically. "You don't have as many kids like I do, Johnny Mack."

Johnny Mack looked at him with a smirk about his face and appeared eager to reply. "That's because I don't care to do all that fuckin' like you do, Mickey. It's nothing but a sport for you, it seems. But for me, it's a pastime."

They all had to laugh behind Johnny Mack's humorous remark.

"But seriously though, Johnny Mack … you too, Hound. I take this to be some type of sign or something. And not only that, I ain't been happy with myself of late. My life hasn't turned out to be anything. I can't sell H forever. And I don't wanna go on this way. Take a look at Don Angelo on that TV set there," he pointed. "The man got plenty of money … plenty of power … and plenty of respect from people at all levels of life. However, all that shit ain't gonna amount to nothing behind that wall in prison. He is seventy-something years old. And more than likely, gonna take his last breath while incarcerated. I'm not tryna go out like that. Not me!" Mickey emphatically stated.

"So, what are you really tryna say to us, Mickey?" Hound asked as he looked at his cousin, wanting a direct response. Preferably, words that were straight and not complicated to understand.

"Okay. So, what I'm really tryna say to you both is that once we get rid of the product that's left, I'm done. I'mma wash my hands, hang up my gloves, and leave it all alone at that point," Mickey stated. His voice clearly indicated how serious he was.

"You got to be bullshittin', right?" Johnny Mack was the first to retort.

"What ail you, Mickey? You a'ight?" Hound let out.

"I've had too many close calls, y'all. I've walked a greased tightwire for far too long. I've got the graveyard on one side of it, and the goddamn chain gang on the other. Not to mention how tired I am, man. I really am. That thing down in Georgia with Frank, was the ticket I needed to get out and walk clean. And now, seeing Don Angelo in those cuffs, and knowing he ain't gonna see not nary 'nother day out here in this free world, is enough to convince my black ass to get the hell on. While I'm ahead. To retire as a winner. Not a loser."

Mickey couldn't have expressed himself any better than he had. He essentially revealed the desires of his soul with his words. And he couldn't any longer be tempted otherwise. Not by Johnny Mack, not by Hound. Not even by Satan himself in that regard.

***

The real reason why Mickey had serious intentions to get away from the life of dope dealing was because his oldest daughter Rachel, and all his kids by JoJo, began to show resentment towards him in more than one way. It's one thing for little boys to show scorn or hatefulness towards a father behind their absence from their lives. However, it's another for the girls to do so. No man would want this. It strikes and hurts differently. To a deeper degree. Especially so when the girls brag about how much better a stepfather or a mother's "boyfriend" even takes better care of them than their own father. That there is enough to make the world's most strung-out junkie, go clean and remain drug free, or a notorious deadbeat, become a great father.

Mickey's transformation began to take root and develop that day, at the sight of Don Angelo being taken away in handcuffs on the news.

Johnny Mack and Hound showed total reluctance to change. They refused to even think and talk like Mickey had. Never mind the fact of them coming close to contemplating an end to a life in the streets.

A wedge was being put between Mickey and those two behind him voicing a decision to exit the world of illegal dealings. And as time passed, the gap was subject to widen. Nothing would be the same moving forward.

Chapter 30

A Few Months Later...

Mickey eventually left drug dealing alone for good. He took the profit money from the last batch of the supply and did right by his kids as intended. He opened multiple trust accounts and thoroughly funded them to benefit each of his seven children. Mickey also bought up several housing and commercial properties throughout Philly and also down in Georgia. The majority of the real estate was renovated and resold. He did hold onto many of them as well. Families in need were helped by him, and he'd sincerely come to realize that there was a better way to go about living life in a legitimized way. And make money while he was at it. The man made it a priority to embrace it all. This adjustment became a winning formula for Mickey. One he was willing to take a chance to grapple with.

The relationship between him and the young lady he had in his life, the lovely Sparkle, became more intimate and praiseworthy. She was twenty-five at the time and Mickey, thirty-eight. Sparkle had no kids and badly wanted a few. Due to her downing birth control pills throughout the times of the past, she wasn't able to become impregnated by Mickey at any time in the affair. Now with her being out on the streets and holding obligation to the commitment she enjoyed with Mickey, the time was at hand to start a family, atop her desire to be a wife.

A recent visit to the doctor revealed she carried Mickey's eighth child. Sparkle was six weeks pregnant. This was brought to Mickey's attention. They hadn't long finished eating dinner and were seated on the couch watching TV. It was affirmed by Sir Alfred Hitchcock, a favorite of Mickey's, *Psycho*. She was situated closely by Mickey's side. He had an arm wrapped around her in a show of affection. The warmth from the heat of the house and their bodies created a cozy comfortable occasion. It was the month of December, and it was cold out that day. Only one week before the Christmas holiday.

"Mickey," Sparkle called out his name in a sensual manner.

He turned his head to face her. The two locked eyes. "Yeah. What's up, babe?" he responded.

"I got a few things on my mind I wanna talk to you about."

"Go ahead. I'm listening."

"I'm your girlfriend, right? Your young girlfriend, that is. And someone who loves you dearly. Someone you love dearly as well."

Mickey smiled at the words she said. He enjoyed the thought of being nearly forty, with a middle, twenty-something-year-old cute female he was in love with.

"You're right, sweetheart. I do love you dearly. But where are you going with this? I'm curious to know."

"Where I'm going with this is here. I'm tired of simply being your girlfriend, Mickey. I'm ready to be Mrs. Savage, you know. It's been a long time coming," Sparkle said, then patiently awaited to know how he would respond to what she's related.

"You say you're ready to be my wife, huh? That you're to be Mrs. Savage. And guess what? I'm ready for you to be all that as well. But the situation I got going on with—"

"Josephine. Your kids' mom. That's a situation you could easily resolve whenever you want to, Mickey," she cut in to say. "I know all about it. Opposite the bits and pieces, you've told me."

"Oh! You do?"

"Yes, Mickey ... I do."

"And how is that?" "Because ... me and JoJo have done a lot of talking between the time. Probably more than you'll ever know. We actually talk all the time. She had me to make a promise that I wouldn't say anything to you of what she and I got going on. Not until the time was right for me to do so." "And why you feel like this is the right time? Of all the times there's been?" he questioned.

"It's because ... we have a special gift on the way. One that's to last a lifetime. Not just over the holiday season," Sparkle said to Mickey and caressed her belly at the same time, displaying a wide loving smile. She gazed deeply into his eyes while laying across his lap.

"For real, baby?" Mickey let out ecstatically.

"So for real, baby," Sparkle confirmed.

"Number eight for me."

"And number one for me."

The two continued to smile and glow about the face while locking eyes with one another. Sparkle had a few additional teasers on the mind she wanted to share with Mickey.

"Mickey, look. My intention is to give you the best version of me ... all of who I truly am and everything I have to offer. And at the same time, I also think that this is the right time to do JoJo the justice she's long asked of you and finally sign off on those divorce papers she needs you to. That way, her and ... Winston ... can continue on with what they have and go on to get married. It's only right that you do," Sparkle stated.

"To be honest, sweetheart. To me, it sounds like you and JoJo may be good friends now. How true is that?"

"It's a lot of truth to that. And yes, we are. A woman would always want to know as much as she could about the next woman, who so happens to be in a relationship with the father of her kids. She would want to know who her children are around. Luckily, y'all kids, all take a liking to me. And now, me and JoJo are closer to one another because of such," Sparkle explained.

"Well, that's good to know, sweetheart. And my word to you is that, I promise, when the opportunity is there for me to do so—probably when you give birth to our baby—I'll go through with the divorce process and let JoJo go on about life with her Winston. And I can do the same with you … my Sparkle. And when is your due date about?"

"Around late August."

"That's good to know. And while we speaking in terms of birthdays, JoJo has one coming soon. I always buy her something. As you know."

"Her birthday on Christmas, right?"

"Yep, and I assume she let you know that too, huh?"

"Mickey. We're good friends now. So of course she did. I adore and respect Josephine, and, she does me. We may be two of a kind. What you think?"

"Y'all similar in a lot of ways. But I'm tryna figure out what y'all got going on? What y'all tryna do to me," he said with a smile, revealing teeth in the process.

"So, if you must be placed on notice, what we're tryna do is, be the ladies in your life you have kids by, and help you come to the understanding that, the pleasure that you love, is expensive to maintain. You got expensive taste. And JoJo and I are young. You managed to get us hooked on you at an early age," Sparkle expressed.

"So, that's what it is! I gotta pay a luxury tax for the pleasure I love?" he uttered, followed by a smile.

"Mm-hmm! And pay you shall do. By continuing to take care of us the way you have. If not better."

"No doubt, I can do that, baby. Doing so is now the best part for me," Mickey responded.

They talked further and watched TV. Mickey had plenty of planning to do, along with preparation for a new baby that was on the way. Also, he somewhat thought in a positive way about the fact of Sparkle and JoJo being cool and close like they were. This wasn't so regarding JoJo utilizing Sparkle and her pregnancy, to move him faster to divorce her. Mickey was so caught up over JoJo whether he wanted to admit it or not. And truth be told, he basically didn't know how to fully move on without her still having his last name. Even with someone else in his life.

Mickey was salty over the fact that JoJo ditched him for a white guy, leaving him butt-sore and in his feelings in the process. It wasn't that JoJo's love for the man had faded. It hadn't. Mickey refused to change at the time. And security and assurance were what she badly wanted. And rightfully so, having to raise five kids in a world of uncertainty.

A peaceful divorce, and going separate ways, was indeed the right direction to take. And to JoJo, Winston proved to be the better man of the two and provided a realistic future for the kids. The likelihood of their success under Winston and living in New Hampshire was higher than it would be with their father and living in Philly. There was nothing to debate about that.

***

Meanwhile...

Johnny Mack, Hound, Frank, Stone, and an additional band of Black Mafia brethren, were able to make progress in the drug business, opposite the fact of Mickey calling it quits and making an exit. The top guys of the French Connection operating in Philly, were introduced to those of BMF. Business began. However, for it to continue, the French Connection demanded Black Mafia to remain in line alongside the men Don Angelo left in position. This was his son, Angelo II. He now heard the family appointed the cousin Rocco, Hound's friend and business partner, to serve as underboss. Rocco's mother Connie was Don Angelo's sister. Tony, Rocco's brother, was made head of security. The indictment and arrests dealt a heavy blow to the Marconi family. Nonetheless, they were able to rebound and make a positive stride.

In keeping true to who he was as a man when it came to his word, the money Mickey owed Don Angelo for those kilos of heroin provided on consignment, he paid to Angelo II. Also, he passed over an additional one hundred thousand to the son, to go towards the legal fees Don Angelo needed to pay for the team of lawyers assembled to represent him. Not that he owed Don Angelo any money or had to do such a thing. It was the fact that Mickey knew and understood how far in relations and in life a genuine gesture could carry someone. And especially so in the world of power and influence.

Don Angelo had a lot of this he could pass on to whom he so pleased, and Mickey put himself in position to receive what Don Angelo had to offer. It's not about what you know. But rather who you know. Don Angelo still had high ranking officials on his payroll dotted all over Philly. These connections were in various municipal principalities of the government. He was made aware of Mickey's kind act.

As both the Marconi and Black Mafia families moved forward, Johnny Mack and Angelo Jr. developed a bond and conducted business in a way like Don Angelo and Mickey had. Equally the same, everything of the underworld Don Angelo had going on, he left to the son. Mickey did this with his cousin. He'd made a wise decision about what to do with his life. This was a good thing coming from a sometimes foolish and reluctant man.

With Mickey nearing forty, he wanted to remain alive and free, to see his kids grow to become adults. And in return, he hoped to be blessed with grandkids. This became his only hope. And to have this as a realistic thing, Mickey began to do something he hadn't done since the times of him being a little boy. He got back to kneeling on his knees, put his hands together, and bowed his head humbly to pray. This was evident proof that no doubt about it, Methuselah "Mickey" Savage, was now a changed man. He was proud of himself over the fact. There was every right to be. Why not?

Epilogue

Two Years Later...

Between the time, Mickey was sure to do the right thing by JoJo and finally signed off on the divorce papers she'd long wanted him to. She and Winston married and continued to live their lives in New Hampshire.

Sparkle gave birth to a son. She and Mickey named him Gerald. In addition, Sparkle also began to place demands on Mickey to marry her. She was ready to be a wife. Mickey wanted the same, but he felt no need to rush at the time, being that he had another expensive wedding that he needed to be paid for, and he wanted to place more focus and attention on this one than the second marriage he was to have.

Mickey's oldest of all, Rachel, was engaged to her long-time boyfriend. She wanted her father, and all her siblings there in Miami to be involved in the events of her special day. Of course, Mickey was to be the one to give his daughter to the husband in the traditional wedding sense, and this meant something to Mickey to have the privilege. He'd never done such a thing before, be in a wedding, let alone have the honor of ceremony go through his dictation. Not even at his own marriage to Josephine.

He bought a minivan for him, Sparkle, and all six young ones he had. They traveled to Florida, checking into a hotel once they arrived. Rachel's wedding was to be this coming Saturday, the second week of June 1971. She would soon become Mrs. Buster Casey. As for him, dude was a cool, slim, dark-complexioned cat with a tall frame and a lot of charisma. A really smooth guy who had a way with words. Mickey took a liking to him. The two were similar in many ways. The occasion turned out to be only the second time he'd had all of his kids together with him at one time. Rachel and Elijah hadn't seen their siblings since they were very young. They were growing. And quickly. Mary was now twelve, soon to be thirteen. She adored her big sister and had intentions to be just like her.

Rachel and Buster were a beautiful couple. Everyone who showed up to celebrate their love and bond, showered them with gifts and affection. Of all people, Mickey blessed them the most, as he should have. He felt really good about himself in the fact he was alive, healthy, and free, and afforded himself the opportunity to pay every penny necessary for his daughter's wedding, giving her over to the groom. Life was wonderful for Mickey. It had been a long time coming. Nonetheless, he made it.

***

Weeks Later...

News got back to Mickey about Don Angelo unfortunately being found "Guilty" on all counts of the indictment. Apparently, the jury of his peers agreed with the prosecutor and did their civil duty by putting the top mobster Marconi away. Forever.

Dolan testified against Don Angelo in a malicious and vehement manner. The most damning of his ratting was related to a murder he'd committed years prior on Don Angelo's orders. Dolan recalled detailed accounts. Before trial began, he took the authorities to the burial site where he'd dumped the body. The skeletal remains of not one, but two people were discovered. They were of the guy who was marked for death, and a girlfriend he was with at the time he met his fate. The identities of the bodies were confirmed through dental records. Don Angelo Marconi Sr. received life multiple times over and would never see the light of day again. Mickey could do nothing but shake his head behind the revelations. This was the perilous end result of life as a mobster. Don Angelo accepted what came his way. Life had to go on.

***

With Mickey out of dope-dealing and no longer involved in the streets, he saw no need to have security by his side as he had in times of the past. Likewise, he no longer carried a pistol on his immediate person. The one he did have was kept locked in the glove compartment of his car. If a situation was to present itself, he wouldn't be able to get to it in time. And in his mind, there would be no life-or-death situation anymore. He was not in the streets or the game any longer. But what about his past in those elements? He gave this no thought. And even with him being out of the way, he still belonged to Black Mafia, and made the decision to be one of the designated leaders. This last part was what the potential rival and streets recognized and knew him as … Don Mickey Savage. Not as a "retired" Don.

There were bloodthirsty vicious young cats in and about the hood, who were looking for any and every opportunity to make a name for themselves and rise in rank in whatever clique they represented. And, Mickey Savage, "the head nigga of Black Mafia," as he was recognized in the streets, was only another name of a nigga, that could be put on a ticket just like anybody else. A drop in a bucket. And at any time, Mickey's ticket could get pulled, leaving him vulnerable to being touched in the process.

In the black ghetto of north Philly, a notorious territory called "the Badlands," no one was off limits. Not babies. Not kids. Not old folks. Disabled persons. Not anybody. When the words "no one was off limits" are emphasized here, it's absolute. Not even the president of the country was, if he tinkered around too long out of place. And at the time, Richard M. "Tricky Dick" Nixon, was in office.

Mickey made an exit from one of the bars he owned in north Philly—The Frontier. Its location was near 18th and Masters. There was a meeting that took place between him and the people he put in charge of running the joint. Mickey picked up money on this night. Mickey kept ten thousand or more on him throughout weekend days. It was on a Saturday. Business was good for all the ventures he had up and going. Profit from the drug operation paid off for him. He also laundered money for Johnny Mack and Hound.

When Mickey had gotten a few steps from the front door of the bar and walked towards the new model Chevy Corvette he'd recently bought, a hooded figure appeared, draped in dark colored apparel. Fleece material. The athletic built male was in Mickey's blindside spot, to his right. He came up from behind. Suddenly, he took action swiftly.

Boom!

A deafening gunshot rang out from a high caliber pistol. Mickey was hit in the hind leg. He went down hard to the pavement. He bellowed in agony from the pain.

Boom! Boom!

Two more shots were fired, hitting Mickey in the right hip and shoulder. He rolled onto his back to face the gunman and attempted to have a look at who it was seeking to end his life. Only a glimpse of the ski mask worn by the assailant was observed. Mickey's vision wasn't long held.

Boom!

Another round was let off. The blinding flash from the barrel altered Mickey's sight. He suffered a slug to the upper torso area. Around the liver.

Boom!

Another round for good measure. He was hit in the chest. Mickey blacked out.

The hitter then ran Mickey's pockets and took all he had. There was fourteen thousand in cash and an expensive ink pen given to him by Don Angelo. It was solid gold with a small diamond resting at the top of the cap.

Mickey's assailant then yanked his alligator skin shoes from his feet, along with the matching belt being pulled from the loop of his pants. These were additional items of profit to benefit from. He then kicked Mickey in the face and ran off into the night, while his victim was in the throes of death from the attack.

To Be Continued...

COMING SOON IN THE SERIES

SAVAGE FAMILY EMPIRE 3
Respect

Lock Down Publications and Ca$h Presents
Assisted Publishing Packages

Due to an increase in the price of services we have increased our prices. The prices below reflect the price increase as of 11/1/24.

BASIC PACKAGE	UPGRADED PACKAGE
$699	$1000
Editing	Typing
Cover Design	Editing
Formatting	Cover Design
	Formatting
	Upload eBooks to Amazon
	Upload Paperback to Amazon
ADVANCE PACKAGE	**LDP SUPREME PACKAGE**
$1,400	$1,700
Typing	Typing
Editing (line editing/content)	Editing (line editing/content)
Cover Design	Cover Design
Formatting	Formatting
Copyright Registration	Copyright Registration
Proofreading	Proofreading
Upload eBooks to Amazon	Set up Amazon Account
Upload Paperback to Amazon	Upload eBooks to Amazon
	Upload Paperback to Amazon
	Advertise on LDP's Amazon and Facebook Page

***

Other services available upon request.
Additional charges may apply

Lock Down Publications
P.O. Box 944
Stockbridge, GA 30281-9998
Phone: 470 303-9761
Email: lockdownpublications@gmail.com

Submission Guideline

Submit the first three chapters of your completed manuscript to ldpsubmissions@gmail.com. In the subject line add **Your Book's Title**. The manuscript must be in a Word Doc file and sent as an attachment. Document should be in Times New Roman, double spaced, and in size 12 font. Also, provide your synopsis and full contact information. If sending multiple submissions, they must each be in a separate email.

Have a story but no way to send it electronically? You can still submit to LDP/Ca$h Presents. Send in the first three chapters, written or typed, of your completed manuscript to:

LDP: Submissions Dept
P.O. Box 944
Stockbridge, GA 30281-9998

DO NOT send original manuscript. Must be a duplicate. Provide your synopsis and a cover letter containing your full contact information.

Thanks for considering LDP and Ca$h Presents.

NEW RELEASES

BLOODLINE OF A SAVAGE 1-3
THESE VICIOUS STREETS 1-3
RELENTLESS GOON 1-3
BY PRINCE A. TAUHID

THE BUTTERFLY MAFIA 1-3
BY FUMIYA PAYNE

A THUG'S STREET PRINCESS 1&2
BY MEESHA

CITY OF SMOKE 3
BY MOLOTTI

GET IT IN SLUGS 1 &2
BY B. STALL

STANDING ON HER BUSINESS 1&2
BY DG SANTANA

STEPPERS 1,2&3
THE REAL BADDIES OF CHI-RAQ
BY KING RIO

THE LANE 1&2
BY KEN-KEN SPENCE

THUG OF SPADES 1&2
LOVE IN THE TRENCHES 2
CORNER BOYS
BY COREY ROBINSON

TIL DEATH 3
BY ARYANNA

THE BIRTH OF A GANGSTER 4
BY DELMONT PLAYER

PRODUCT OF THE STREETS 1-3
BY DEMOND "MONEY" ANDERSON

NO TIME FOR ERROR
BY KEESE

MONEY HUNGRY DEMONS 1-2
BY TRANAY ADAMS

HUB CITY MENACE 1-3
BY J. WHITE

A THUGGISH PASSION 1&2
LAND OF DA HOOLIGANZ 1-4
KILLAZ ON STANDBY 1&2
BY IRA B.

FO'EVA ROLLIN 1&2
BY ASSA RAYMOND BAKER

THE LEVEL UP 1&3
BY LUXURY KING

Coming Soon from Lock Down Publications/Ca$h Presents

IF YOU CROSS ME ONCE 6
ANGEL V
By Anthony Fields

A THUGS STREET PRINCESS 3
By Meesha

CORNER BOYS 2
By Corey Robinson

THA TAKEOVER
By Keith Chandler

BETRAYAL OF A G 2
By Ray Vinci

SAVAGE FAMILY EMPIRE 1&2
SOULLESS GOON 1,2&3
THE DIRTY SIDE OF MONEY 1,2&3
By Prince

FOR MY ENEMY'S SAKE
AMBITIONS OF A SLIDER
FRESH OFF DA PORCH
By IRA B.

THE TRUCKLOAD 1-4
TIPPIN' THE SCALES 1-3
BAD BITCHES WIT GUNZ 3
PROBLEM SOLVED 2
By Christopher "Diesel" Hornezes

Available Now

RESTRAINING ORDER 1 & 2
By **CA$H & Coffee**

LOVE KNOWS NO BOUNDARIES 1-3
By **Coffee**

RAISED AS A GOON I, II, III & IV
BRED BY THE SLUMS I, II, III
BLAST FOR ME I & II
ROTTEN TO THE CORE I II III
A BRONX TALE I, II, III
DUFFLE BAG CARTEL I II III IV V VI
HEARTLESS GOON I II III IV V
A SAVAGE DOPEBOY I II
DRUG LORDS I II III
CUTTHROAT MAFIA I II
KING OF THE TRENCHES
By **Ghost**

LAY IT DOWN I & II
LAST OF A DYING BREED I II
BLOOD STAINS OF A SHOTTA I & II III
By **Jamaica**

LOYAL TO THE GAME I II III
LIFE OF SIN I, II III
By **TJ & Jelissa**

IF LOVING HIM IS WRONG…I & II
LOVE ME EVEN WHEN IT HURTS I II III
By **Jelissa**

PUSH IT TO THE LIMIT
By **Bre' Hayes**

BLOODY COMMAS I & II
SKI MASK CARTEL I, II & III
KING OF NEW YORK I II, III IV V
RISE TO POWER I II III
COKE KINGS I II III IV V
BORN HEARTLESS I II III IV
KING OF THE TRAP I II
By **T.J. Edwards**

WHEN THE STREETS CLAP BACK I & II III
THE HEART OF A SAVAGE I II III IV
MONEY MAFIA I II
LOYAL TO THE SOIL I II III
By **Jibril Williams**

A DISTINGUISHED THUG STOLE MY HEART I II & III
LOVE SHOULDN'T HURT I II III IV
RENEGADE BOYS 1-4
PAID IN KARMA 1-3
SAVAGE STORMS 1-3
AN UNFORESEEN LOVE 1-3
BABY, I'M WINTERTIME COLD 1-3
A THUG'S STREET PRINCESS 1&2
By **Meesha**

A GANGSTER'S CODE 1-3
A GANGSTER'S SYN 1-3
THE SAVAGE LIFE 1-3
CHAINED TO THE STREETS 1-3
BLOOD ON THE MONEY 1-3
A GANGSTA'S PAIN 1-3
BEAUTIFUL LIES AND UGLY TRUTHS
CHURCH IN THESE STREETS
By **J-Blunt**

CUM FOR ME 1-8
An LDP Erotica Collaboration

BLOOD OF A BOSS 1-5
SHADOWS OF THE GAME
TRAP BASTARD
By **Askari**

THE STREETS BLEED MURDER 1-3
THE HEART OF A GANGSTA 1-3
By **Jerry Jackson**

WHEN A GOOD GIRL GOES BAD
By **Adrienne**

THE COST OF LOYALTY 1-3
By **Kweli**

BRIDE OF A HUSTLA 1-3
THE FETTI GIRLS 1-3
CORRUPTED BY A GANGSTA 1-4
BLINDED BY HIS LOVE
THE PRICE YOU PAY FOR LOVE 1-3
DOPE GIRL MAGIC 1-3
By **Destiny Skai**

A KINGPIN'S AMBITION
A KINGPIN'S AMBITION II
I MURDER FOR THE DOUGH
By **Ambitious**

TRUE SAVAGE 1-7
DOPE BOY MAGIC 1-3
MIDNIGHT CARTEL 1-3
CITY OF KINGZ 1&2
NIGHTMARE ON SILENT AVE
THE PLUG OF LIL MEXICO 1&2
CLASSIC CITY
By **Chris Green**

A GANGSTER'S REVENGE 1-4
THE BOSS MAN'S DAUGHTERS 1-5
A SAVAGE LOVE 1&2
BAE BELONGS TO ME 1&2
A HUSTLER'S DECEIT 1-3
WHAT BAD BITCHES DO 1-3
SOUL OF A MONSTER 1-3
KILL ZONE
A DOPE BOY'S QUEEN 1-3
TIL DEATH 1-3
IMMA DIE BOUT MINE 1-6
DYING FOR LIKES
By **Aryanna**

A DOPEBOY'S PRAYER
By **Eddie "Wolf" Lee**

THE KING CARTEL 1-3
By **Frank Gresham**

THESE NIGGAS AIN'T LOYAL 1-3
By **Nikki Tee**

GANGSTA SHYT 1-3
By **CATO**

THE ULTIMATE BETRAYAL
By **Phoenix**

BOSS'N UP 1-3
By **Royal Nicole**

I LOVE YOU TO DEATH
By **Destiny J**

I RIDE FOR MY HITTA
I STILL RIDE FOR MY HITTA
By **Misty Holt**

LOVE & CHASIN' PAPER
By **Qay Crockett**

TO DIE IN VAIN
SINS OF A HUSTLA
By **ASAD**

BROOKLYN HUSTLAZ
By **Boogsy Morina**

BROOKLYN ON LOCK 1 & 2
By **Sonovia**

GANGSTA CITY
By **Teddy Duke**

A DRUG KING AND HIS DIAMOND 1-3
A DOPEMAN'S RICHES
HER MAN, MINE'S TOO 1&2
CASH MONEY HO'S
THE WIFEY I USED TO BE 1&2
PRETTY GIRLS DO NASTY THINGS
By **Nicole Goosby**

LIPSTICK KILLAH 1-3
CRIME OF PASSION 1-3
FRIEND OR FOE 1-3
By **Mimi**

TRAPHOUSE KING 1-3
KINGPIN KILLAZ 1-3
STREET KINGS 1&2
PAID IN BLOOD 1&2
CARTEL KILLAZ 1-3
DOPE GODS 1&2
By **Hood Rich**

THE STREETS ARE CALLING
By **Duquie Wilson**

STEADY MOBBN' 1-3
THE STREETS STAINED MY SOUL 1-3
By **Marcellus Allen**

WHO SHOT YA 1-3
SON OF A DOPE FIEND 1-4
HEAVEN GOT A GHETTO 1&2
SKI MASK MONEY 1&2
By **Renta**

GORILLAZ IN THE BAY 1-4
TEARS OF A GANGSTA 1/&2
3X KRAZY 1&2
STRAIGHT BEAST MODE 1&2
By **DE'KARI**

TRIGGADALE 1-3
MURDA WAS THE CASE 1-3
By **Elijah R. Freeman**

SLAUGHTER GANG 1-3
RUTHLESS HEART 1-3
By **Willie Slaughter**

GOD BLESS THE TRAPPERS 1-3
THESE SCANDALOUS STREETS 1-3
FEAR MY GANGSTA 1-5
THESE STREETS DON'T LOVE NOBODY 1-2
BURY ME A G 1-5
A GANGSTA'S EMPIRE 1-4
THE DOPEMAN'S BODYGAURD 1&2
THE REALEST KILLAZ 1 3
THE LAST OF THE OGS 1-3
By **Tranay Adams**

MARRIED TO A BOSS 1-3
By **Destiny Skai & Chris Green**

KINGZ OF THE GAME 1-7
CRIME BOSS 1-4
By **Playa Ray**

FUK SHYT
By **Blakk Diamond**

DON'T F#CK WITH MY HEART 1&2
By **Linnea**

ADDICTED TO THE DRAMA 1-3
IN THE ARM OF HIS BOSS
By **Jamila**

LOYALTY AIN'T PROMISED 1&2
By **Keith Williams**

YAYO 1-4
A SHOOTER'S AMBITION 1&2
BRED IN THE GAME
By **S. Allen**

TRAP GOD 1-3
RICH $AVAGE 1-3
MONEY IN THE GRAVE 1-3
CARTEL MONEY 1&2
By **Martell Troublesome Bolden**

FOREVER GANGSTA 1&2
GLOCKS ON SATIN SHEETS 1&2
By **Adrian Dulan**

TOE TAGZ 1-4
LEVELS TO THIS SHYT 1&2
IT'S JUST ME AND YOU
By **Ah'Million**

KINGPIN DREAMS 1-3
RAN OFF ON DA PLUG
By **Paper Boi Rari**

THE STREETS MADE ME 1-3
By **Larry D. Wright**

CONFESSIONS OF A GANGSTA 1-4
CONFESSIONS OF A JACKBOY 1-3
CONFESSIONS OF A HITMAN
CONFESSIONS OF A DOPE BOY
By **Nicholas Lock**

I'M NOTHING WITHOUT HIS LOVE
SINS OF A THUG
TO THE THUG I LOVED BEFORE
A GANGSTA SAVED XMAS
IN A HUSTLER I TRUST
By **Monet Dragun**

QUIET MONEY 1-3
THUG LIFE 1-3
EXTENDED CLIP 1&2
A GANGSTA'S PARADISE
By **Trai'Quan**

CAUGHT UP IN THE LIFE 1-3
THE STREETS NEVER LET GO 1-3
By **Robert Baptiste**

NEW TO THE GAME 1-3
MONEY, MURDER & MEMORIES 1-3
By **Malik D. Rice**

CREAM 2-3
THE STREETS WILL TALK
By **Yolanda Moore**

THE STREETS WILL NEVER CLOSE 1-3
By **K'ajji**

LIFE OF A SAVAGE 1-4
A GANGSTA'S QUR'AN 1-4
MURDA SEASON 1-3
GANGLAND CARTEL 1-3
CHI'RAQ GANGSTAS 1-4
KILLERS ON ELM STREET 1-3
JACK BOYZ N DA BRONX 1-3
A DOPEBOY'S DREAM 1-3
JACK BOYS VS DOPE BOYS 1-3
COKE GIRLZ
COKE BOYS
SOSA GANG 1&2
BRONX SAVAGES
BODYMORE KINGPINS
BLOOD OF A GOON
By **Romell Tukes**

CONCRETE KILLA 1-3
VICIOUS LOYALTY 1-3
BLOODY MONEY BAGS
By **Kingpen**

THE ULTIMATE SACRIFICE 1-6
KHADIFI
IF YOU CROSS ME ONCE 1-3
ANGEL 1-4
IN THE BLINK OF AN EYE
By **Anthony Fields**

THE LIFE OF A HOOD STAR
By **Ca$h & Rashia Wilson**

NIGHTMARES OF A HUSTLA 1-3
BLOOD AND GAMES 1&2
By **King Dream**

GHOST MOB
By **Stilloan Robinson**

HARD AND RUTHLESS 1&2
MOB TOWN 251
THE BILLIONAIRE BENTLEYS 1-3
REAL G'S MOVE IN SILENCE
By **Von Diesel**

MOB TIES 1-7
SOUL OF A HUSTLER, HEART OF A KILLER 1-3
GORILLAZ IN THE TRENCHES
OOPS CRY TOO 1&2
THE DAUGHTER OF A CARTEL BOSS
By **SayNoMore**

BODYMORE MURDERLAND 1-3
THE BIRTH OF A GANGSTER 1-4
By **Delmont Player**

FOR THE LOVE OF A BOSS 1&2
By **C. D. Blue**

KILLA KOUNTY 1-5
TENDER
By **Khufu**

MOBBED UP 1-4
THE BRICK MAN 1-5
THE COCAINE PRINCESS 1-10
STEPPERS 1-3
SUPER GREMLIN 1-4
A GANGSTA'S SON
By **King Rio**

MONEY GAME 1&2
By **Smoove Dolla**

A GANGSTA'S KARMA 1-5
By **FLAME**

KING OF THE TRENCHES 1-3
By **GHOST & TRANAY ADAMS**

BAD BITCHES WIT GUNZ 1&2
PROBLEM SOLVED
By "Christopher Diesel" Hornezes

QUEEN OF THE ZOO 1&2
By **Black Migo**

GRIMEY WAYS 1-3
BETRAYAL OF A G
By **Ray Vinci**

XMAS WITH AN ATL SHOOTER
By **Ca$h & Destiny Skai**

KING KILLA 1&2
By **Vincent "Vitto" Holloway**

BETRAYAL OF A THUG 1&2
By **Fre$h**

COUNTDOWN OF A KILLA 1&2
SEX, MURDER AND GOD 1&2
GUNS DOWN, BOTTOMS UP 1&2
By Lo-Life

THE MURDER QUEENS 1-7
By **Michael Gallon**

FOR THE LOVE OF BLOOD 1-4
By **Jamel Mitchell**

SAVAGE FAMILY EMPIRE 2 | PRINCE A. TAUHID

THE BUTTERFLY MAFIA 1-3
SALUTE MY SAVAGERY 1&2
By **Fumiya Payne**

THE LANE 1&2
By Ken-Ken Spence

THE PUSSY TRAP 1-5
By **Nene Capri**

DIRTY DNA
By **Blaque**

SANCTIFIED AND HORNY
by **XTASY**

BOOKS BY LDP'S CEO, CA$H

TRUST IN NO MAN
TRUST IN NO MAN 2
TRUST IN NO MAN 3
BONDED BY BLOOD
SHORTY GOT A THUG
THUGS CRY
THUGS CRY 2
THUGS CRY 3
TRUST NO BITCH
TRUST NO BITCH 2
TRUST NO BITCH 3
TIL MY CASKET DROPS
RESTRAINING ORDER
RESTRAINING ORDER 2
IN LOVE WITH A CONVICT
LIFE OF A HOOD STAR
XMAS WITH AN ATL SHOOTER